Vespers in Vienna

Books by Bruce Marshall

FATHER MALACHY'S MIRACLE
THE WORLD, THE FLESH, AND FATHER SMITH
YELLOW TAPERS FOR PARIS
VESPERS IN VIENNA

Vespers in Vienna

by BRUCE MARSHALL

HOUGHTON MIFFLIN COMPANY BOSTON

1947

AUTHOR'S NOTE

The attention of readers, and especially of those who served contemporaneously with the author in Austria, is drawn to the fact that the events described in this novel, and the characters who perform them, are entirely imaginary. In order to make this quite clear, and to avoid giving offence to hard-working senior and junior officers whom the author has every reason both to like and to respect, the method of military government, as regards both the British Zone of Austria and the quadripartitely administered city of Vienna, has been left deliberately vague or confused. Such foibles and frailties as are exhibited by the persons who take part in this invention originated in the brain of the author, who, being imperfect himself, is only too able to manufacture imperfection.

London, 1947   BRUCE MARSHALL

The selection from "Tommy," from *Departmental Ditties and Ballads and Barrack-Room Ballads* by Rudyard Kipling, copyright 1892, 1893, 1899, 1927 by Rudyard Kipling, is reprinted by permission of Mrs. G. Bambridge and Doubleday & Company, Inc.

PRINTED IN THE UNITED STATES OF AMERICA BY
KINGSPORT PRESS, INC., KINGSPORT, TENNESSEE

For

'Il y a peu de vrais chrétiens, je dis même pour la foi. Il y en a bien qui croient, mais par superstition; il y en a bien qui ne croient pas, mais par libertinage: peu sont entre deux.'

Pascal: *Pensées sur la Religion et sur la morale.*

~~~~~~~~~~

'Confessons la vérité: qui trieroit de l'armée, mesme légitime, ceulx qui marchent par le seul zèle d'une affection religieuse, et encores ceulx qui regardent seulement la protection des loix de leur païs, ou service de prince, il n'en scauroit bastir une compagnie de gentsd'armes complette.'

Montaigne: *Essais.*

I

BRIGADIER CATLOCK had signalled for Colonel Nicobar to come up to Vienna at once and help him to rehabilitate Austria, and, deep in the panting heart of Rome, the colonel was having one last read through the papers in his in-tray just in case somebody from a higher level than the brigadier should have ordered him to go to Athens instead. On that morning in August, 1945, however, there were only the customary reams of routine, some of them slightly anachronous, owing to the channels through which they percolated being silted up by custom and fatigue.

'Transport, motor radiators of,' the colonel read without astonishment, 'anti-freeze measures will no longer be taken.' 'Campaigns will, as far as possible, be arranged to coincide with non-malarious seasons. . . . Only the female mosquito desires blood. Owing, however, to the impossibility of distinguishing between the male and the female mosquito, it will be necessary to destroy ALL mosquitoes.' The colonel, accustomed by thirty years' service to the scriptures of strategists and quartermasters, did not smile. Nor did he smile when he read in a newspaper which parroted to perfection the imperfections of the home press: 'Atom Bomb, Greatest Ever, Used on Japs,' and, 'Sky Hotels Planned to Fly World Routes.' For, despite his calling, the colonel was reflective enough to wonder sometimes whether the 'four freedoms' could ever be secured by dynamite and whether progress was synonymous with propulsion.

No such uncertainties appeared to exist in the mind of Brigadier Catlock when, five minutes later, his voice came crackling through from Vienna, on a rickety line:

'Catlock here, Nicobar. Get my signal?'

'Yes, sir.'

'In that case, what are you doing in your office? You ought to have been on your way hours ago.'

'Your signal only came last night, sir, and I had all sorts of arrangements to make.'

'Full colonels oughtn't to have to make arrangements, Nicobar,' the brigadier's voice said, with a rasp of reprimand. 'That's what they've got gee two's for. What's the answer to that one, eh?'

'There is no answer to that one, sir,' the colonel said, knowing that there was no use arguing with brigadiers, especially when they were younger than you were. When he had been a company commander at Mons, Brigadier Catlock had still been at Marlborough, sucking sticky sweets and carving his initials on desks; and, when he had been a major at the War Office, the brigadier had been a company commander in the Buffs, splitting his infinitives in one of Empire's most forlorn fortresses. That was what the brigadier found it so hard to forgive him; nothing failed like success.

'There isn't, is there?' The brigadier made his voice more pleasant, disposed towards generosity now that he had been put wrongly in the right. 'Well, I still don't see any reason why you shouldn't come by road provided you don't stop to swan in Venice.'

'You may count on me, sir,' the colonel said.

'I hope so, Nicobar,' the brigadier said. 'There's a hell of a flap on here about everything from gasworks to foreign exchange and everybody seems to be making a nonsense of everything as usual.'

The brigadier rang off, leaving the colonel in a very bad temper indeed.

'Where's Senior Subaltern Quail?' he shouted at the closed door.

Sergeant Moonlight came in and stood blinking at the colonel.

'Did you say anything, sir?' he asked.

'I didn't say; I shouted,' the colonel said. 'I asked where Senior Subaltern Quail was.'

'I expect she's downstairs aving a cup of tea, sir,' Sergeant Moonlight said.

'You do, do you?' the colonel snorted. 'Do you know this, Moonlight? I sometimes think that if it hadn't been for the British soldier's inveterate habit of swilling his belly with tea in the middle of the morning and the afternoon, the War would have been won two years sooner. And the danger's not over and done with yet by any means. Some day you may have reason to realise the truth of my words, Moonlight, down a salt mine in Siberia.' The colonel's wrath sank as quickly as it had risen, because he didn't really like being rude to people, especially to his subordinates who couldn't answer back. 'Sorry for being stuffy, Moonlight,' he said, 'but if there's one thing I can't stand, it's slackness, because it's slackness that's going to lose us our civilisation.' He smiled at the sergeant, wondering what it must feel like to wonder what it must feel like to be an officer.

'Perhaps it's not slackness Miss Quail being out to 'ave a cup of tea, sir,' Sergeant Moonlight said. 'Perhaps it's just fate.'

'Perhaps you're right,' the colonel said. 'Perhaps it's just fate.'

They stood smiling at each other in silence, at ease in their unspoken loyalty to a semi-understood cause. In the twenties and thirties, when other men had been thinking about making money, the colonel and the sergeant had both been soldiers, thinking about being soldiers; and in the fifties, when other men were again thinking about being soldiers, the colonel and the sergeant would still

4

be soldiers, protecting the profit-making poltroons while they prepared the next catastrophe, from which the soldiers would again have to extricate them. Across their meditation the bells of Rome pealed out in the hot noonday, reminding men that Mary was for ever blesséd.

'Is Oliness the Pope singing *Abide With Me*, sir,' Sergeant Moonlight said.

'Sometimes I take rather a dim view of the Holy Father and sometimes I don't,' the colonel said.

'I was born a Methodist, but my father was an Evangelitical, but when I joined the army I gave up my religion,' Sergeant Moonlight said.

The door opened and Senior Subaltern Quail entered. She had long silky black hair which shone in a sheen in the sunlight. She wore an open khaki shirt, a short khaki skirt, and was smoking a cigarette in a green holder. When he had first met her, the colonel doubted whether she was quite a lady, because she neither swore nor drank too much; but the vehemence with which she was pursued by officers of the Brigade of Guards and the Twenty-First Lancers, as well as the authority with which she could express her political and philosophical misconceptions, had speedily reassured him.

'Niente sugar in the coffee this morning,' Senior Subaltern Quail said. 'Been flagged to the Eyties, I expect.'

'Where's Twingo?' the colonel asked. 'The briga-dier's rung up already. We ought to have started hours ago.'

'I haven't a clue, but I expect he's saying good-bye to the marchesa,' Senior Subaltern Quail said, draw-ing in the little carmine smudge of her italicised lips. 'She can say what she likes about sticking up for democracy now, but I'll bet she was no end of a fascist when Mussolini was around.'

'The trouble with the Eyties is they've got no cultural education, ma'am,' Sergeant Moonlight said.

'The way they behave at times you'd think they owned the country,' Senior Subaltern Quail said.

'Are you ready to start, Audrey?' the colonel asked. He would much have preferred to call her 'Miss Quail,' because he was old-fashioned enough to believe that Christian names ought to be used by people only when there was intimacy between them; but in the Eighth Army everybody seemed to call one another 'Bob,' 'Bill,' and 'Mabel,' and it would have been priggish not to observe a con-vention which had been consecrated by military success. 'We'll bundle the kit in the fifteen hundred-weight and drive round to the marchesa's and pick up Twingo,' he said.

Audrey nodded dully and redundantly pigmented her face, gazing moodily into a small silver moon of mirror. For Audrey was in love with Twingo, whose real name was Major McPhimister, D.S.O., M.C.

Observing her distress, the colonel patted her kindly on the shoulder.

'I shouldn't let it get me down, if I were you,' he said.

Audrey gave him a brief smile of gratitude

The Colonel put his red hat on his red hair and marched away downstairs and Audrey and Sergeant Moonlight followed him. The colonel had lost his left arm on the Menin Road in the last war, but he carried his stick in his right hand with a grand swing to make up for it. On his way downstairs he remembered when he'd been in love for the first time at sixteen and how she had had long loose brown hair falling down her back and how he'd taken her to see Mr. and Mrs. Sidney Drew at the cinema and how he'd walked home with her through the dark in silence afterwards. At the door of her house she'd drawn off her silly pudgy little blue woollen glove and held out a shy hand. 'Good night, Mr. Nicobar,' she had said. 'Thank you so much for taking me out. I've enjoyed myself immensely.' 'Good night, Miss Dale,' he had said. He had never seen her since, and sometimes he thought that he must still be in love with her, because for him she still wore long brown stockings and a black beaver hat with the brim turned up.

When they got downstairs, they found that their

kit had already been loaded onto the fifteen hundredweight. The three orderlies who had been loading it sat on the steps in the sun with expressions of concentrated witlessness on their faces, and did not stand up as the colonel approached.

'Middens!' the colonel roared. 'Who's the senior private here? Upon my soul, I never saw such a lot of unmannerly louts in all my life.' For the colonel could swear with vehemence and originality when he was angry, spilling his oaths in a pretty pepper and disproving Talleyrand's definition of swearing as the means whereby the inarticulate gave themselves the impression of eloquence.

The soldiers sprang to attention and stood staring in front of them with terrified docility. Impressed by their attrition, the colonel remembered that these men had been through the battles of North Africa and Italy and that when they returned to England the civilians would show them little gratitude. In the third-class compartments of suburban trains and the cheap seats in provincial cinemas their heroisms would moulder into anonymous mediocrity. It had happened after the last war and it would happen again after this war. The smooth men, the safe men, the men that crucified Christ for a block of debentures, the men of majorities would ride again in limousines with their tinned women.

'You see, it's not me that I want you to salute,'

he explained, trying to put into words the thoughts which were riding across his soul. 'It's not because I'm a colonel; it's because I represent authority. And it's authority that makes the world go round, even a democratic world. Only it's got to be a *good* authority. And that's precisely what we try to have in England: a good authority. A *good* authority, so that we may govern wisely a *good* people.' The colonel floundered as he tried to explain the problems that had baffled Aristotle, Plato, and Saint Thomas of Aquin to six golliwog eyes frosted with fright. 'And if the people don't respect authority, authority, even good authority, can do nothing for them. You must try to get it into your heads that discipline's going to be as necessary for Britain in peace as in war. And then there's the question of giving a good example in an ex-enemy country.' From the perplexity on their faces, the colonel saw that it was no use continuing. Whatever he said to them, as soon as he had turned his back, they would start calling him a bastard. 'All right, then; don't let it happen again,' he concluded lamely.

Sergeant Moonlight jumped onto the back of the fifteen hundredweight to make sure that the Italians didn't steal the kit or unscrew a wheel when they stopped in a traffic block, and the colonel and Audrey got into the staff car. Audrey sat in front with the driver so that she could go on smoking without annoying the colonel. The three orderlies stood to grim attention as they drove out of the courtyard.

Round the Piazza Esedra they drove, with the American soldiers watching the children paddle in the fountains, down the Via Nazionale, past grubby priests and barefooted Franciscans, past the crumbling glory of Santa Maria in Cosmedin, past the Forum and the Coliseum, up the Avventino and past Santa Sabina and San Anselmo, on and out to where the marchesa had her flat.

The marchesa was not on her balcony, but they could hear her through the window, squealing away at Twingo: 'Cattivo, cattivo maggiore, maggiore, che porco maggiore.'

'The fate that is worse than death and more pleasant than plum pudding,' Audrey said as she climbed the stairs with the colonel.

The marchesa herself opened the door. 'Colonello, colonello! You have arrived just in time!' she cried. 'The maggiore is a very knotty buoy, much more porco than Ciano, although I really had not much to do with him because I am always being very democratica since oh such a long time.'

The lusts of the flesh were one of the many subjects about which the colonel had never been able to make up his mind, disliking equally the condemnations of clergymen and the licence of lechers. He supposed that the answer was, as often, the *via media:* love without sex was as unthinkable as sex without love, and both were compulsions to which men and women submitted according to their spirit, clumsily or with beauty.

'Twingo,' he said, 'this is quite intolerable. The brigadier's just been on the telephone. He's asking why we haven't started hours ago.'

'Oh, colonello, but you must not be angry with my porco maggiore because he's such a nice porco maggiore,' the marchesa said.

'Signora, I am not upbraiding the major for dalliance, but for neglect to comply with an operational order,' the colonel said.

'But the war is over, colonello, and the English are going to be ever so kind to us poor Italians who were misled by that scoundrel Mussolini, so I am thinking that there is no more need for operational orders,' the marchesa said, shaking her syrup-pudding head.

'As far as we are concerned, the war has only begun, and we ought to have started hours ago,' the colonel said. He knew that it was really his fault more than the major's that they hadn't started hours ago, but that only made him angrier, although he knew that the expression of his distemper was unjust. 'Come on, Twingo, and get your good-byes over.'

'And I hope you haven't forgotten to leave a tin of sardines or a spare tyre on the mantelpiece,' Audrey said, not too loudly and not too quietly.

11

II

DRIVING ALONG ROUTE TWO the colonel's hand
that wasn't there began to pain him, as it often
did when he sat in a draught, or when the heat
was excessive, or a change of weather was about
to take place. Sharp little red-hot stings shot
down his non-existent fingers, nipping in stabbing
needles of fire. The colonel never liked to talk
about these pains to people unless they had lost
an arm or a leg too, because he was afraid that
they wouldn't understand. Consequently, when
Senior Subaltern Quail discovered, five miles out of
Rome, that she had left her gold powder compact
behind in the hotel and asked permission to turn
round and drive back and collect it, the colonel
was too intent upon concealing his agony to give
expression to his discontent. He managed, it is
true, to find time between jabs to reflect that that
sort of thing hadn't happened at Festubert, when
they had run wars properly, without women. But
the curves that were Audrey hadn't existed then,
although they now intruded their geometry all over
his car, so that she wouldn't have understood his

comparison even if he had been able to express it, and she always said that she was bored by the last war, anyhow.

On the way back into Rome, the colonel didn't think about Audrey, and he tried not to think about his pain because he considered it foolish still to be hurt by a wound which had happened nearly thirty years ago. 'Just a boy,' the full colonel surgeon had said to the major surgeon when they had stopped at the foot of the hospital bed in Rouen, watching him lie there with his arm newly off, and he had felt terribly angry and insulted because he had been twenty-three and a half and had known that he was really quite old. 'Don't worry, old chap,' the full colonel surgeon had said, misinterpreting his look of distress, 'the girls'll still love you just the same'; and the colonel had smiled then because he had wanted the girls to go on loving him; and the girls had, from the blonde V.A.D., who had used to teach him to tie his tie with one hand, to the girl with the raven hair in the white dress whom he had picked up in Felixstowe and who had written down her address for him on the flap of a cigarette packet which he had afterwards thrown away by mistake. Thinking about girls was one of the colonel's favourite ways of forgetting the pain in his fingers, that weren't there, and now he thought about them hard, all the way down the road back into Rome, past the basilica of Saint John

13

Lateran, thinking how much prettier they had been than they were now, chasing the ghosts of long ago frocks.

The hotel at which they had been billeted was now empty because most of the military governors had flown to Vienna two days previously, but Audrey crossed the deserted lounge with her wonted willowy wiggle, throwing out her right hip and protruding her chin. The colonel and Twingo sat in the car and watched her in silence, because the colonel was sulking with Twingo for having gone to visit the marchesa and Twingo was sulking with the colonel for having rebuked him for having gone to visit the marchesa. Soon, however, Audrey, having failed to find her compact in her room, was back again in the doorway, reprimanding the porter in her curried Italian.

'Tutta Italia molto libidinosa,' she shouted at him and got back into the car and slammed the door.

This time as the car sped out of Rome, it was the colonel and Twingo who were friendly together and Audrey who was sulking. The pain was beginning to go from the colonel's fingers and he didn't need to think about girls any longer, so he thought about Twingo instead.

Twingo had had, as the phrase was, a good war. A Forty-Second Highlander, he had been taken prisoner in 1940 with the Fifty-First Division at Saint-Valéry, but had escaped and returned to

England via Spain and Miranda. Then he had fought in North Africa, and afterwards he had done secret things behind the German lines in North Italy, for which he had won a D.S.O. and an M.C. and bar. The colonel had a D.S.O. and an M.C. and bar too, and, although he had won them in a démodé war, he liked to think that they formed a link between himself and Twingo whose daring was still new enough to be brave. He supposed that Twingo, who was a regular soldier, would be a general one day, tolerating the young majors of the next war as he tried to tolerate the young majors of this. It was impossible, of course, to tell what Twingo thought about the war and the reasons for which it had been waged, because Twingo rarely talked about politics or religion or literature, but walked about behind his great smasher of a desert moustache as though he were thinking only of next week's N.A.A.F.I. spirit ration, as indeed was possible. All the same the colonel hoped that there was a streak of reflection in Twingo somewhere, because in a sense serving soldiers were priests, and there were very few priests left in the world these days, with everybody out for pelf in their pockets.

At first they drove along the road at a terrible lick, because they were anxious to overtake the fifteen hundredweight, which the colonel had told to trundle on ahead, so as not unduly to delay their joining up with Brigadier Catlock gnawing at his in-basket in Vienna. The colonel didn't like driving quickly, and from time to time he stuck an angry face out of the car window, bawling an imprecation in Hindustani at lorry drivers who manoeuvred their vehicles in too close proximity to his. Then on a clear stretch of road he relaxed and started to find pleasure in thinking about how miserable he was going to be in Vienna, because being in Vienna meant meeting another bunch of ox-faced soldiers he had never seen before, and the colonel didn't like meeting strangers, because it always seemed to take a long time to get to know them and then there was generally nothing to know. But that was what an army career was like in the main, rising from second lieutenant to general and never hearing or saying anything that mattered, although of course soldiers were much better than stockbrokers, because soldiers were chaps and stockbrokers weren't.

The colonel was on the point of dropping off to sleep on this thought, when the driver applied his brakes with a jerk, and the car screeched to a standstill, throwing the colonel's belly heavily against the seat in front and his nose into Senior Subaltern Quail's hair. It took the colonel several seconds to realise what had happened, and by that time Twingo was out of the car, and standing in the road roaring physiological monosyllables at the driver of an eight hundredweight Chevrolet, which was drawn broadside on across the road at a corner. The colonel

16

jumped out of the car and strode out to join Twingo, brandishing his stick.

'You horrible little swashbuckling R.A.S.C. buccaneer!' he shouted. 'Sticking your great snout across a road round a blind corner like that!' And the notice by the side of the road only incensed the colonel further because it frightened him as well:

DEAD MEN

GET

NO

LIAP

GO SLOW

'Heaven shame your perverse and obdurate heart,' he said.

'Yes, sir,' the driver of the eight hundredweight Chevrolet said.

'Hooky, by God!' a voice from inside the Chevrolet said, and a ripe red face beneath a riper red hat peeped out from the window of the Chevrolet. 'I think I'd have recognised that vocabulary anywhere.'

The colonel, too, would have recognised the ripe red face anywhere, for it belonged to Colonel Humphrey Omicron, with whom he had been at Dunmere, Sandhurst, the Battle of the Somme, and the Delhi Durbar.

'Oh dear,' said Colonel Nicobar, 'I never knew it was you, Blinker.'

17

'Nonsense, Hooky,' said Colonel Omicron. 'My fault, of course. Got the damned truck stuck in the ditch when we broke off for lunch and now she's made a nonsense of it and won't go at all. Well, Hooky, what about giving me a lift as far as Florence, and then I'll see if I can get an L.A.D. to run out and tow this chap in?'

Although he forced himself to extend the invitation with a smile, Colonel Nicobar was not pleased at the prospect of driving all those kilometres in his friend's company, because he wanted to unravel idly threads of interesting memories and he knew from past experience that no officer in His Majesty's Brigade of Guards could talk balderdash more fluently than old Blinker.

There was a bit of a squash with three of them sitting in the back of the car, but Colonel Omicron did not seem to mind, and he started in right away.

'Come to think of it now, don't think I've seen you since we were both up before the G.O.C.-in-C. for that last spot of bother,' he said.

'You mean about the iron rations,' Colonel Nicobar said.

'No, I mean about the floor polish,' Colonel Omicron said. 'When Carruthers Twiggle Carruthers in the Skins — that is not Boggle Carruthers in the Fogs, because that's his brother — when old Twiggle indented for twenty tins of floor polish and some babu wrote down twenty *tons* of floor polish and the D.A.D.S.T. kicked up about the transport and we both got a rocket from the old man.'

Colonel Nicobar said that he remembered, but he wasn't quite sure. There had been, in his military career, so many spots of bother and so many rockets that he sometimes found it hard to disentangle them and to remember by whom and when he had been rebuked, by Field Marshal Haig in the last war or by Field Marshal Montgomery in this.

'And what are you doing now?' Colonel Omicron asked.

'I'm on my way to join Catlock in Vienna,' Colonel Nicobar said. 'He's a brigadier now, you know.'

'Well, upon my word,' Colonel Omicron said. 'And what's he a brigadier about?'

'Military government, I believe, in fact I know,' Colonel Nicobar said.

'Hasn't a clue, of course,' Colonel Omicron said. 'Never did have. I remember him as subaltern in the Green Howards.'

'Buffs, you mean.'

'No, Hooky, I mean the Green Howards. Lieutenant C.M.V. Catlock didn't transfer to the Buffs till 1927 and he was a captain then.'

'Perhaps you're right. What you doing, Blinker?' Colonel Nicobar asked the question out of politeness, because he didn't really care what Colonel Omicron did, so long as it wasn't with him.

19

'Oh, I'm off to see a cad in Padua about a job in Welfare,' Colonel Omicron said.

Twingo did not attempt to take any part in the conversation because he was only a major and majors didn't talk to full colonels they didn't know unless the full colonels whom they didn't know spoke to them first. Audrey, however, although only a senior subaltern, was restricted by no such etiquette, because Audrey was a pretty girl and even full colonels were human.

'I believe I knew a girl who knew you at A.A.I., sir,' she said, slanting her green eyes at him and fluttering her eyelids. 'A girl called Mary Smith. It's funny my remembering her because of course I'll never forget her.'

'The Gloucestershire Smiths, of course?' Colonel Omicron said.

'Shropshire, sir, I think,' Audrey said.

Colonel Nicobar smiled sideways at the notices painted on the ends of houses which read, MORTE AL MONARCO, and, through a smear of transparent whitewash: UN POPOLO FORTE NON PUO VIVERE SENZA SPAZIO. He could read a little Italian, but it was Colonel Omicron who was amusing him and not the sight of the communist and the fascist slogans side by side. For it was obvious from the way that he was popping his eyes that old Blinker was falling for Audrey in a big way; and a few kilometres further along the dusty road Audrey was no longer

calling him 'sir,' and was telling him all about
Rome and how the frescoes in the Sistine Chapel
were fun, and how she had told the Pope that she
didn't think the apostolic succession really mattered.
Colonel Nicobar didn't listen much after that, but
fell contentedly asleep, rocked to rest by the sound
of their voices and the car as it swooped through
the summer day.

III

THEY ARRIVED in Vienna four days later, on a Sunday, driving through battered streets, with few pedestrians on the pavements except batches of grubby Russian soldiers plodding about with their hands in the pockets of their big balloon trousers. Although he had seen lorry loads of them while driving through the silent Soviet Zone, the colonel continued to watch them with interest, because it was the first time that he had observed the Red Army at close quarters, and he wanted to see if there was anything in their eyes or their bearing which might enlighten him about their philosophy. They did not appear, however, apart from the peculiarities of their livery, very different from other soldiers, trudging along in a disinterested despond.

In the course of his life the colonel had seen many soldiers with that look of apathy on their faces: French soldiers, Italian soldiers, American soldiers, and, in this latter war, even British soldiers. He supposed that this mask of deliberate thoughtlessness was imposed by their calling, which consisted for the most part in being led up the garden

22

by politicians, who spewed great words at them about honour and glory and history, which generally meant exports, oil, and doing the other bigmouthed chap in the eye. For they couldn't all be fighting all the time for civilisation, art, and religion, and even the least reflective of them must, on occasion, observe that his opponents were spurred to brave the flying iron by the same sooth eructing from different lips. All the same, the colonel had always respected soldiers, because he had shared their misery in battles and knew that their discipline, applied by good men for good purposes, was the only thing that could save the world. He did not, however, know what to think of the Russian soldiers, because he did not know what they were thinking about.

Brigadier Catlock, however, knew exactly what to think of the Russians when they met him at the Park Hotel, where the brigadier was staying.

'Capital chaps at bottom, although they're not a bit like us really, but then one must remember that their outlook is entirely different,' the brigadier said, as he led the way into the lounge which was filled with brass hats having tea in the company of a horde of yapping high-class young women whom the colonel rightly concluded to be their personal assistants. 'They do you well, too. Gave us a crackerjack of a lunch the other day. Lashings of vodka and no heeltaps. Of course, they're a little bit difficult to do business with. Say they'll turn up at meetings and don't, because it's the anniversary of some revolution or other, and that sort of thing.' The brigadier led the way to the table which had been specially reserved for him, conscious that his one silver lock of hair and his badges of rank made him doubly conspicuous. 'Still, I don't believe they want another war any more than we do.'

'It's all up with us if they do, sir,' the colonel said. 'There's no such thing as welfare in the Russian Army. There's only the cause, and they don't care a damn how many men they sacrifice to attain it. Old Blinker Omicron told me the other day that in the Soviet Army they don't publish casualties below the rank of lieutenant-colonel. And he ought to know if anybody does because he was Colonel G.S.I. with 386 Div at one time.'

'Blinker's a dim bulb if ever there was one,' the brigadier said. 'And in my opinion his being Colonel G.S.I with 386 Div was largely responsible for the way the Hun held us up at the Gothic Line. No, no, Nicobar, the Soviets are all hunky-dory, you can take it from me.'

The colonel had better reason than the brigadier for knowing that the Russians were hunky-dory, for once, in Jugoslavia, he had watched a Soviet division capture in a few hours from the Germans a bridge which the 386th Division could not have taken in under a week. Down the hill those flaxen-

24

haired boys had marched, laughing and singing, and the bullets had come tearing at them, smashing their tibias, cracking their femurs, opening their bellies, gouging their eyes, grounding them, scorching them. As, through his field-glasses, the colonel had watched them swept from the bridge into the river, it had not seemed to him that they could really be suffering, as he himself had suffered in 1914, with the big angry red thing up against him, and he had had to make an effort of will to understand that each of these boys had died his own death, smash up against the Christ he didn't believe in, with his bowels gushing out over his boots as he thought for the last time of his mother, and with his hair still young in the sun. And still others had come on, laughing and singing, as they marched to kill and to be killed by other boys with lineless faces, because it was sweet and decorous to die for one's country. Yes, the Russians were hunky-dory all right, provided they were fighting on the same side as you were.

Senior Subaltern Quail, who hadn't had much opportunity for conversation since Colonel Omicron had dropped off to see his cad friend at Padua, thought that it was about time that she expressed an opinion.

'After all, I expect it's really a question of politics, isn't it, sir?' she said, exquisitely fluttering her eyelashes.

The brigadier turned to regard her with interest.

'You've put the whole matter in a nutshell,' he said. 'Politics, that's what's at the bottom of the matter.'

'It's what's the matter with the whole world, sir,' Twingo said, for Twingo could be intelligent when he liked. 'Communists and fascists instead of Catholics and Protestants. The old fanaticisms blowing the old unreasoning hatred through new channels.'

The colonel rather liked Twingo when he talked like that, because it made him think that he wasn't the only soldier who bothered about ideas.

'And yet it isn't such an unhealthy division, because after all, it is more healthy to squabble about theories than about possessions,' the colonel said. 'It's a nonsense to say that men should be Britons and Frenchmen and Russians first and communists and Christians and fascists afterwards. They should be communists and Christians and fascists first, and Britons and Frenchmen and Russians afterwards, for it is only by making a philosophy and not a nation prevail that we shall ever attain universal peace. That's why this war's decided nothing, really, because it was fought for national survival and not for philosophical penetration.'

'Trouble with you, Hooky, you read too many books,' the brigadier said. 'Democratic principles are the only thing that matter, and as for religion I know the padres have done a good job of work, but who goes to church these days, anyway?'

The colonel did not ask the brigadier to define what he meant by democratic principles and neither did Audrey, who was now all out to capture the brigadier's interest.

'I gave up going to church years ago,' Audrey said. 'For religious reasons, of course.'

'That's funny, Miss Quail; so did I,' the brigadier said, his eyes beginning to cloud with a hungry desert look.

The colonel ceased to listen while the brigadier and Audrey set about discussing the daring original-ity of not going to church in an age when nobody else did. He had seen Audrey at work before and he knew by heart all her manoeuvres. Instead he looked round the room at the faces of the men who were to be his new colleagues. Most of them were brigadiers, although some of them were full colonels and the airenvolk were there as well, clustered in groups all by themselves, because they had won a different war. Their expressions were for the most part unreflective as they sat cramming slices of cake beneath their monster moustaches.

The colonel didn't think that he was going to like any of them very much, and wondered, not for the first time, why the only times in his career when he had not felt proud of being a soldier were when he had been among a crowd of other soldiers. Perhaps, though, the faces he was watching felt the same way about his, because even brigadiers were alone in their

27

bodies, with their souls screwed away down inside, for nobody but themselves to see. He wished, though, that he could have gone on serving with the friends he had known in the last war: Armitage who had been killed at La Bassée, Gregory who had been sniped at Givenchy, Sullivan who died in his arms in front of Cambrin, all so brave, all so vanished.

The sight of the last-war medals on a few breasts cheered him into hoping that he might find among his new colleagues at least a few with whom he might be able to exchange ideas, but for the most part the campaign ribbons he saw began with the 1939–45 star and the faces above them were much less lined than his own. So bright and arrogant they were, these new ribbons, the North Africa, the Italy, and the France-Germany star, but soon the deeds they symbolised would fade, too, as their colours in the sun, and they would become hallowed for all men, because they would stand for acts no longer tarnished by journalists.

'Bigglewick,' the brigadier was saying into the tilted wheel of Audrey's ear, 'remember him well. We were at Singapore together in twenty-five and old Biggles swiped the last bottle of gin while I was up changing. Hollow legs that chap had. Gordon's gin too. Married a title, they tell me, or someone with good sound connections: anyway, her mother died in the Ritz.'

'Thundering mediocrity really,' Audrey said.

'Biggles? Of course, he hasn't a clue,' the brigadier said.

'Daddy says that General Barbecue-Bolton — he's a great friend of the family — swears he once saw him sucking an orange on the grandstand at the Aldershot tattoo,' Audrey said.

'Doesn't astonish me in the least,' the brigadier said. 'Still, I flatter myself I'm a man of the world, and what with the Gestapo and all those boring stories of atrocities one reads of, I must say nothing shocks me very much any more.'

'They weren't boring to the chaps who suffered them, sir,' the colonel said.

'I beg your pardon, Hooky,' the brigadier said.

But the colonel knew that the brigadier had heard quite well what he said. He also knew that he was going to bore them by what he was going to say next, but he was going to say it all the same, even although Audrey was already yawning in anticipation and showing the horseshoe of her lower teeth studded round her pink tongue.

'That's just the trouble really,' he began, hoping to hammer the ideas that were so real to him behind the brigadier's cold grey eyes. 'Nobody's shocked by anything any more: we're not shocked by deceit, cruelty, lust for power, faithlessness, money-grubbing. Indeed, we accept it as inevitable that each and every one of our fellow men should be impelled only by selfishness. Well, sir, let me say that it's

stupid of us not to be shocked, because the continua-
tion of our civilisation depends precisely upon our
ability to be shocked. That's why we fought the
war, or perhaps it would be more correct to say
that that was for what they told us we were fighting
the war. The reason given us for fighting the war
was that we were shocked by cruelty. The extension
of that cruelty to millions instead of thousands of
individuals in no way lessened our obligation to go
on fighting the war for the same reason for which
we were told that we entered it, because each man,
woman, or child that suffers and dies suffers and
dies alone, his pain unmitigated by the commonalty
of his weal. Well, we've fought against that cruelty
and won; but if our winning is going to mean anything for humanity at all, there are two things that
we must not do: the first is to say that that cruelty
was excusable because it was universal; and the
second is to imagine that corruption of motive and
intention must not be fought against as well.'

The colonel's reasoning sounded so irrefutable to
himself that he thought it must sound irrefutable to
the others as well, but he was wrong, because
Twingo was the only member of his audience whom
he saw looking at him with any sort of understanding and even he appeared a little perplexed.

'So many long words, Hooky,' the brigadier said.
'I've always been a great chap for simplicity myself.'

'Well, sir, if you don't mind, I see quite a few

friends who seem anxious to speak to me,' Audrey said, and she rose and smoothed out her khaki skirt.

Audrey spoke the truth. The brigadiers, colonels, lieutenant-colonels, and majors were all gazing at her with bulging eyes. The brigadier, the colonel, and Twingo sat and watched her for a few moments as she moved about among the tables, bestowing the benediction of her pigments upon the restive soldiery.

'Well, Hooky, I expect I'd better explain the form a little,' the brigadier said.

'Yes, sir,' the colonel said.

'Yes, sir,' Twingo said.

'As you know, the directive of His Majesty's Government is that we are to rehabilitate Austria,' the brigadier said.

'Yes, sir,' the colonel said.

'Yes, sir,' Twingo said.

Brigadier Catlock explained the form, and for one whose main task had hitherto been the destruction of enemy forces he explained it quite well. All Austria had been divided into four zones to be administered by the Russians, the Americans, the French, and the British respectively: the Russians were to govern the province of Burgenland and Lower Austria, the Americans Upper Austria and Salzburg, the French the Tyrol and the Voralberg, and the British Carinthia and Styria; Vienna itself was to be divided up into its Bezirke, each of which would be administered by one of the four Powers, the only exception being the first Bezirk or the Innerestadt, which would be administered quadripartitely. The trouble with such a procedure was, the brigadier rightly stressed, that, while it satisfied the aspirations and jealousies of the four Powers, the different motives inspiring each Power rendered uniformity of government almost impossible. In their zone the Russians were openly pursuing a policy of revenge and despoliation and the French remembered that two years previously Austrian troops had been occupying France; in the British and American zones, on the other hand, the inhabitants were ruled with clemency and justice, perhaps with a little bit too much clemency, because the brigadier didn't feel that the Austrians had been as innocent of war guilt as it was now the fashion to pretend. In any case, it was, in the small proportion in which the colonel and himself would be concerned in the military government of Austria, their duty to attempt to put the country back on its feet again. All this the brigadier said quite well and the colonel listened attentively, because he knew from past experience that young Catlock could always state a problem neatly. Then the brigadier began to talk about team spirit, and the colonel listened less attentively, because he hated clichés.

'Well, I don't know about you chaps, but I could do with a quicky,' the brigadier said.

Lined along the bar the other high-ups, having just finished their tea, were having quickies, too, and Audrey was having one with them, moving saucily from group to group. Their uniforms were multiform: some wore bush shirts without medal ribbons and others khaki drill shirts with medal ribbons; some wore their badges of rank sewn onto their shoulder straps, some had their badges of rank sewn on khaki envelopes slid over their shoulder straps, and others wore metal pips and crowns stuck in. Lined along the bar they stood, loving themselves, pouring martinis and sherry and vermouth down their important funnels — 'good chaps chiefly because they weren't better chaps. Brigadier Catlock stopped still in his tight little shorts and watched them with distaste.

'These fellows and their ridiculous khaki shorts,' he said.

Colonel Nicobar nodded. Even soldiers were no longer what they were: once more the decency of war was beginning to slip away from them and leave in its place the beastliness of peace.

A waiter came up and said 'good evening' and the brigadier said 'Guten Abend' back. Then the brigadier ordered the drinks. They all three sat, not knowing what to say to one another and watching another brigadier trying to cram a whole slice of melon into his mouth at once. Audrey's voice came piercingly across a brief general silence as, glass in hand, she stood telling a wing commander how she intended to treat the Austrians. 'After all, we're conquerors, aren't we?' she said and the wing commander agreed so much that he poured his Tom Collins down his shirt.

'Sometimes I think we didn't deserve to win this war,' Brigadier Catlock said.

'Never mind, sir, we'll lose the next,' Twingo said.

The brigadier laughed. There was another silence during which the colonel wondered whether he could open up his favourite topic about the soldiers on both sides never having really known what they had been fighting about, but decided that he'd better not, as he didn't really know Brigadier Catlock very well.

'There's old Tinkle,' the brigadier said, nodding in the direction of a lanky group captain. 'Let's ask him over: he looks stupid enough.'

Tinkle came over and was introduced as Group Captain Twillingham. Then he sat down and said nothing and went on looking stupid. The silence seemed as though it would last for ever. Then the brigadier laughed and said:

'That reminds me, Nicobar: I forgot to tell you. You and your staff are billeted in a convent: Daughters of the Holy Ghost or something they call themselves. That'll teach you to go blinding and blasting about the place. Nuns and Nicobar. Ha, ha, damned funny, what!'

IV

COLONEL NICOBAR didn't think it funny at all,
because he liked doing as he pleased in his mess,
and turning on the wireless as loud as he wanted,
and shouting at the top of his voice when one of
the invisible seers said something more than ordinarily foolish, and he was afraid that such conduct
might not go down very well in a convent.

'Nuns!' he exclaimed bitterly, as with Audrey
and Twingo he rolled in his car down the Mariahilferstrasse towards the Innerestadt where the
Kongregation der Töchter des Heiligen Geistes had
their convent. 'Well, one thing's certain, and that
is that I'm not going to stand any nonsense.'

'I think nuns are fun,' Audrey said. 'I had a
friend who was at a convent once, and really she
said it was wizard and that the nuns were frightfully
broadminded and allowed her to make up as much
as she wanted to and have masses of boy friends call
and take her out, but, of course, she was Church of
England really.'

The colonel said nothing. He was rehearsing
the speech he was going to make to the Mother
Superior, or whatever she called herself. 'Look here,

Madame,' he would say, 'I don't suppose that you like having us here any more than we like being here, but that's no reason why we shouldn't get on well enough together, provided we keep out of each other's way.' And of course there would be religious pictures and statues and things. Well, provided one wasn't too brutal about it, perhaps one could persuade the nuns to put them out of the way and let a chap stick up a decent stag's head instead, and that reminded him that there was good hunting in Austria: chamois and all sorts of things.

The colonel was right: there *were* religious pictures and statues in the convent, and Schwester Kasimira of the Agony in the Garden was dusting one when the colonel rang the front doorbell. The statue was a statue of the Sacred Heart, and it wasn't a very beautiful one either, but that didn't make Schwester Kasimira want to replace it by a stag's head, because she thought that the Lord was beautiful enough as He was, and that statues at best were only approximations, and even if they were ugly, they did point the way to heaven, and that was more than could be said of cinema houses and advertisements which were generally much uglier still and rarely, in her opinion, made any sense at all. Turning from her work, she went quietly to the door and opened it. Behind her pale blue pillows of incense floated in a beam of sunshine,

for Benediction of the Blessed Sacrament had just
been given and the nuns had come out of chapel
and some of the incense had come out with them.

'Guten Abend, Herr Oberst,' she greeted with a
grave inclination of the head.

'Deutsch nicht gut,' the colonel said, saluting
awkwardly.

'Io parlo italiano,' Audrey said, simulating a look
of big-eyed innocence.

'Peut-être mon colonel parle-t-il français,' Schwester Kasimira said.

'Oui, oui,' said the colonel, fluently.

'Eh bien, mon colonel, justement nous attendions
votre arrivée puisque l'on nous l'avait déjà an-
noncée,' Schwester Kasimira said. 'Et si vous
vouliez bien vous donner la peine de me suivre la
Révérende mère voudrait avoir l'honneur de parler
un peu avec vous avant que vous ne gagniez vos
appartements.'

'Eh?' the colonel said.

'I mean that you will perhaps follow me,' Schwester Kasimira said.

They followed her, walking supererogatively on
tiptoe, as though afraid to awaken the saints in
whom they had never believed. Twice in their
progress along the long polished corridor they
passed small groups of nuns, who bowed back at
them gravely. From time to time Schwester
Kasimira kept glancing back over her shoulder and

beckoning them on with a smile, which was in her eyes as well as on her lips, and gliding on again noiselessly on the big beehive of her ample skirt.

'Reverend Mother will be with you soon,' she said as she showed them into a parlour which was bare except for a crucifix, a table, and six uncomfortable chairs. The crucifix had a dried palm leaf folded in the form of a cross stuck under the I.N.R.I. superscription; the palm leaf had been put there on Palm Sunday and would remain there until next Ash Wednesday, when it would be taken out and burned and the ashes smeared on the nuns' foreheads, as a reminder that even their holy bodies must turn again to dust.

'I say, she seems rather a poppet, doesn't she?' Audrey said.

When Reverend Mother Auxilia came into the room, she wasn't smiling as much as Schwester Kasimira, although the sun shining on her glasses gave her an aspect of benevolence. She came in with her hands folded and the rope of her long rosary rattling, gave that serious little bow which the other nuns had given them in the corridor, motioned to them to seat themselves once more and herself sat down. The broad round wheel of her starched white bib kept rumpling up as she spoke and she kept smoothing it down again with her fingers.

'My colonel,' she began in fairly flawless French,

'you and your friends do us Daughters of the Holy Ghost a great honour in electing to live under our roof, and we trust that we shall prove ourselves worthy of that honour.'

'Ce n'est pas nous, madame; c'est le major du town,' the colonel said.

'Anyway, I'm sure it's going to be fun,' Audrey said.

'Perhaps, mademoiselle, not so much fun as you may think,' Reverend Mother Auxilia said. 'You see, our life is a life of prayer, and while you are very welcome here and we shall do all in our power to make your stay pleasant, the life of our community must go on. Oh, I know what you are thinking,' she said, reading behind the self-conscious acquiescence on their three faces. 'You are thinking of how many priests and monks and nuns have prayed in the past and of what little good it seems to have done to the world with this terrible war just over and millions dead and wounded and other millions homeless; but that is perhaps because we have not prayed enough or because sufficient people have not prayed enough: it cannot be because we have prayed, because, if everybody in the whole world prayed sincerely about the right things, there would certainly be no more wars.' She smiled as she said this and became so beautiful that the colonel thought that he could imagine what she had looked like as a young woman.

'Après tout, nous sommes after the same thing as you are,' the colonel said.

'Yes, but are you sure that you are after it so very hard?' Reverend Mother said gently. 'Please do not misunderstand me, but I think that the trouble of the world is this: It has never been easy to obey our Lord's commands, not even in the days when all Europeans were Christians, and did not imagine that, just because they could see planets and stars and the moon at the end of a telescope, Christ had not died for their sins and risen from the dead. That was, my colonel, the great disservice your nineteenth-century materialists did to the world: to make it more difficult to obey the Lord. For there are two ways in which men and women obey the Lord: the first is because of love, and the second is because of fear, and always more have obeyed because of the second reason than because of the first.

'The people who formerly obeyed because of love still obey from love, but those who used to obey because of what they were afraid was going to happen to them in the next world if they didn't, no longer do so, because the clever men have told them that the next world does not exist and that consequently after death there is neither reward of virtue nor chastisement of sin. You may not perhaps think that these things are very important, but if you wish to save European civilisation, you will be foolish not to think so. For the terrible thing about the modern world is that disobedience of God's commandments carries far more widespread consequences than it used to carry. Lust of possession and of power, lying, thieving, stealing, there have always been in the world, but in the Middle Ages their range of effect was less widespread, because man had not yet learned to counsel their practice simultaneously to millions or to destroy simultaneously other millions who resisted their particular disobedience of God because they wished to carry out another themselves.

'In other words, my dear colonel, I am trying to suggest to you that there can be a connection between the rocket bomb harnessed to atomic energy and the private nihilism that there is today in most men's hearts, and that the only way to prevent our cities crumbling for the last time and men and women all over the world dying in a putrid swelling of blackened bodies is for us to turn again and love God with all our heart. So perhaps it is not so foolish as you think for us to pray, although perhaps you have an alternative philosophy to offer?' Reverend Mother Auxilia smiled as she asked this question, perhaps to reassure the colonel that she wasn't just trying to be clever.

'You win, Reverend Mother,' the colonel said. 'I'm afraid I can't tell you the answer to that one.'

'I'm afraid I haven't a sausage either,' Twingo said.

'Well, I'm not going to preach at you any longer, because I am sure that I have talked too much and badly at that,' Mother Auxilia said. 'Do you know, sometimes when I think of the unhappiness of the world, I wonder if priests and nuns are not greatly responsible for men and women not listening and not obeying more. You see, we have such a very wonderful thing to say and we say it so badly. Shall I tell you a truth? Sometimes when I read holy papers I feel like becoming a little worldly myself, because of the big phrases in which big truths are stated. For big truths are most powerful in little phrases — but there I go preaching again, and committing the sin of spiritual pride as well, because I don't express our Lord's wisdom very wisely myself. And now, if you will allow the community and myself to offer you a slight refreshment?'

'But we shall be dining shortly, Reverend Mother,' the colonel said.

'Yes, my colonel, but that will not be our business,' Reverend Mother Auxilia said. 'Our Holy Founder, Saint Walburga of Graz, was always most strict that no stranger should come within our gates and not be nourished. I know that what we have to offer will not be much, but it will be such as we can offer and a token, I hope, of the charity which will always exist between us.'

So the colonel and Twingo and Audrey had to drink weak tea on top of the martinis and sherries they had already drunk; and the whole community came crowding in and watching them like startled penguins as though they, and not the nuns, were the exception to the rule. Schwester Kasimira of the Agony in the Garden, however, soon had them all smiling because she asked the colonel which was the greater, a lieutenant-general or a major-general, and Schwester Michaela of Jesus Found Teaching in the Temple told her not to let soldiers think nuns were as silly as all that and that of course a major-general was greater than a lieutenant-general, because major meant 'greater' in Latin. Then the colonel told her that as a matter of fact she was wrong, and that lieutenant-generals were more important than major-generals, but that she mustn't mind being wrong, because she was quite right about the relation of the words, because the army was a topsy-turvy place, and in any case major-generals were often cleverer than lieutenant-generals into the bargain.

Schwester Michaela smiled and said that she didn't mind how wrong she was and apologized to them all for having committed the sin of spiritual pride, and said that the colonel mustn't really mind the Army being a topsy-turvy place because the Church was often a topsy-turvy place as well, with curates and chaplains often holier than canons and bishops, but of course that wasn't quite the same, because the Lord was there to guide the Church, and

43

although she didn't want to be rude, she didn't think that He had always guided the army in quite the same way. Then the nuns left them and Reverend Mother said that both the nuns and herself would be delighted to see them all later at compline, and Audrey said that she would be delighted, although she was afraid she didn't know what compline was, but she thought it had something to do with praising.

The colonel did not go to compline, but stood leaning out of his bedroom window instead, looking at the lighted windows of the chapel shining through the trees. The nuns were singing and their voices came sweetly across the darkness of the garden:

> *Te lucis ante terminum,*
> *Rerum creator, poscimus*
> *Ut, pro tua clementia,*
> *Sis praesul ad custodia.*

'The trouble about these nuns is that they've no idea what a dirty dog I really am,' he said.

'Quite a fortuitous journey we ad really, adn't we, sir; nothing really appened,' said Sergeant Moonlight, who had come round to see that the colonel was comfortable.

The nuns began to sing the *Salve Regina* and the colonel and the sergeant stood on at the window silenced by the knowledge that they were listening to something holy. The singing ceased, but the chapel windows shone on out on the trees and made the branches look like saints' robes, for the nuns were still praying that God would grant them a quiet night and a perfect end.

Then Twingo came in and was very excited.

'I've been at church, and I've seen the loveliest girl I've ever seen in my life,' he said. 'She was sitting in a sort of special tribune place let into the wall like a box in a theatre. She had a face as cool as alabaster and she wore a big white hat with a thin black ribbon on it and a white dress and long white gloves and she looked awfully cold and proud.'

'Perhaps she'll help you to forget the marchesa,' the colonel said.

Down in the garden the chapel lights went out and the branches of the trees became branches again, but Schwester Kasimira was still moving about in the sanctuary, laying out the altar cards for the next morning's mass, when holiness would have to begin all over again.

V

'Such fascinatingly earthy words the colonel uses at times,' Audrey used to say, and, forgetting his piety of the night before, the colonel was using them now, fluently feeding his discontent into the funnel of the telephone. For one thing, there was as yet no glass in the windows of his new office and the draught was making his fingers that weren't there ache; and, for another, Audrey ought to have been there to answer the telephone, but, as often, she was out, keeping the troops' morale up by consuming iced cakes and coffee in the company of a pop-eyed brigadier.

'Look here, Captain Gideon, or whatever your name is, I don't know you from a bar of soap and I don't know that I want to frightfully,' the colonel shouted, hating his absent hand for hurting so much and himself for getting angry so easily.

Audrey came tiptoeing in with a guilty smirk on her face, looking subcutaneously elated. The pop-eyed brigadier had just offered to give her private lessons in Hindustani and had told her that she mustn't think that he was like the other brigadiers swanning around because what he liked was a Girl with a Mind. Noiselessly she removed the receiver of the parallel telephone from its hook and received the answer to the colonel's blast.

'Quite,' she said. 'I'm sure the colonel will understand perfectly. Yes, tell the general he can come over straightaway. The colonel will esteem it an honour to receive him. Byee.'

'The brigadier is sending a Rumanian general over to see you, sir,' she said to the colonel.

The colonel grunted and rose from his desk and went and stood by the glassless window and tried not to think about how his fingers were hurting him so much. Down in the courtyard a swarm of German prisoners of war was clearing up the rubble into which, during the bombing of Vienna, a part of the building had disintegrated. In untidy pale green uniforms they shuffled about their task, looking neither very wicked nor very virtuous. A few British corporals stood supervising them, and they didn't seem very wicked or virtuous either, but only bored, sharing even the servitude of the vanquished.

The colonel thought, as he had thought in Cologne after the last war, how, when you saw them with their faces growing out of their clothes, little different those who had fought for the wrong looked from those who had fought for the right and how the hair grew in the same way on the heads of the sons of Belial as on the heads of the sons of God. Beside the great round wheel of a lorry a British and a German soldier were showing each other photographs of their families, jerking with their thumbs the syntax of understanding. Watching them, the colonel wondered about war and peace while behind him Audrey sketched a new damp red pout on her lips, in case Rumanian generals should be interested, too, in Girls with Minds.

The Rumanian general, who was accompanied by a Rumanian lieutenant-colonel and a Rumanian major, reacted immediately. Wearing a khaki hat with an enormous crown, he advanced towards Audrey's desk and saluted so energetically that the rows of little metal medals on his chest tinkled in tiny tintinnabulations.

'Mademoiselle, je suis entièrement à votre service,' he said. Audrey stuck up the spikes of her eyelashes, wriggled in her blouse, and shone a beam of understanding on the general.

'Mon général, je suis très fond of the Balkans,' she said.

'Je vois que mademoiselle parle adorablement le français,' the general said.

The colonel, who had frequently assisted at this sort of scene, advanced in bulk from behind his desk to intervene.

'Sir, my name is Colonel Nicobar,' he said.

'My respects, colonel,' the general said. 'My name is General Koposchin and I have with me Lieutenant-Colonel Manoschin and Major Potoschin.'

48

The colonel shook hands with the Rumanian officers who all sat down and went on looking at Audrey's legs, while Audrey herself stared intensely out over the top of the telephone like a sailor trying to sight land.

'My colonel, I have come about a very important matter,' General Koposchin said. 'Sixty thousand Rumanian soldiers who fought against fascism are missing. I have come to enlist the aid of the Pritish to help to find their allies who witnessed so pravely for the ideals of democracy.'

'Mais j'ai toujours geglaubt that Rumania fought contre the Allies,' Colonel Nicobar said. Muddled by memories of so many treacheries, he realized with dismay that he was beginning to forget who had fought against whom and for what. 'I'm right, aren't I?' he asked Audrey.

'Of course, sir,' Audrey said. 'We declared war against Rumania and Hungary the same day. I remember perfectly well because I was lunching with Clarence de Barbizon at the Ritz and Clarence was fearfully interested because Clarence is a communist, although he's not a communist really, but I'll never forget what he said, although I can't remember the exact words now, but I know it was frightfully political.'

'That's just the point,' General Koposchin said. 'Pritain declared war on Rumania, but Rumania never declared war on Pritain.'

'At heart Rumania was neutral,' Lieutenant-Colonel Manoschin said.

'Neutral against whom?' Colonel Nicobar asked.

'Ah, my colonel, there you have it,' General Koposchin said. 'At first Rumania may have been just a little neutral against the Allies, but that was because the rogues who governed her did not understand the brincibles of democracy, but by the end of the war, although she was a too small country to make spectacular gestures, Rumania was being very neutral against Germany.'

'You see, it is all a question of degree,' Lieutenant-Colonel Manoschin said.

'We sometimes think that it is very difficult for Englishmen to understand Continental bolitics,' Major Potoschin said.

'There are, you see, so many nuances,' General Koposchin said.

'Such a lovely word, "nuance,"' Audrey said. 'So literary, don't you think?'

'I see that mademoiselle is an exceedingly cultured young woman,' General Koposchin said.

'I am sure that mademoiselle must be a great reader,' Lieutenant-Colonel Manoschin said.

'De livres très profonds,' Major Potoschin said.

'Comme ci, comme ça,' Audrey said.

The telephone on the colonel's desk rang.

'Nicobar here,' the colonel said.

'Catlock here,' the brigadier's voice said out of a

50

black bottle of invisibility. 'Come over, will you? I want to speak to you.'

The colonel left the Rumanian general and his officers and Audrey to talk about literature and the sixty thousand missing Rumanians who had fought for the four freedoms and walked along the street to the building in which Brigadier Catlock performed military government. Two soldiers, with slovenly disinterest on their unlighted faces, attempted to pass him without saluting and the colonel bawled at them, telling them that they were a disgrace to empire, commonwealth, metropolitan England and Western civilisation, and then was very sorry for them as soon as he had rebuked them, because he knew it wasn't any great shakes being a private soldier, even a victorious one, with fifty cigarettes and a bar of chocolate a week free issue. Then a military band started to play behind the wall of a neighbouring barracks and the colonel threw out his chest and marched proudly, remembering the Menin Road.

'The subject is subversive activities, Hooky,' Brigadier Catlock said when the colonel walked in and saluted. The brigadier was wearing a new khaki drill tunic, and his two rows of medal ribbons were very clean and bright, and he swung round in his chair so that the colonel might notice the smartness of his attire. Then the telephone on his desk went, too, pinging away shrilly. 'No, I have it on the authority of Captain Gideon that the Soviets view with intense disfavour any proposal to introduce the gold standard into Austria,' he said and put down the receiver. 'The subject is subversive activities,' he said again.

'I thought that was the province of G.S.I.(b),' the colonel said.

'Nothing's the province of anybody these days,' the brigadier said, calling the colonel "Nicobar" instead of 'Hooky' to show him that he didn't like being interrupted. 'What do you think I'd be talking about the gold standard for if people had provinces any more? Between you and me I don't know the difference between the gold standard and a bull's knee, and it's fortunate I've got young Gideon to help me because his uncle's a mining engineer. Makes me laugh like a drain when I think of it. We were talking about subversive activities, weren't we? I want you to make that your special job, Nicobar. I want you rigorously to investigate any evidences of subversive activity which you may come across and to apprehend the perpetrators and hand them over to military justice.' The telephone rang again and the brigadier spoke again, trying out a new fierce tone of voice which he had copied from a general in Rome. 'No, the British Red Cross may not get office furniture from Eighth Army,' he said and crashed the receiver down again. 'That chap doesn't know whether he's sitting on a land-mine in Timbuctoo or on top of a bus in the Edgware Road,' he said. 'Subversive activities, Hooky, you've got to crush them ruthlessly.'

'The term "subversive activity" needs definition surely, sir,' the colonel ventured to say.

'You'll be asking me to define "military government" next,' the brigadier said, angry again. 'Look here, Hooky, don't start making mountains out of mole-hills. Every junior commander in the A.T.S. knows these days that "subversive activities" means acting or uttering propaganda against democratic doctrines or principles or whatever you choose to call them.'

'Perhaps the trouble with me, sir, is that I am not a junior commander in the A.T.S.' Colonel Nicobar said. 'Perhaps that's why I don't understand. According to the balderdash talked by the B.B.C. propagandists, democracy means all rights and no duties, freedom to lie in bed reading the *News of the World* on Sunday mornings without having to earn that leisure by six days' previous hard work. According to the hermaphrodites of the microphone, all the practices and customs of the past are reactionary and rotten and all the blueprints for the future are progressive and sound. Well, I for one don't believe it. Even if there have been abuses in the past, the fact of their existence does not incline me to believe that the habits and conventions wrought painfully out of centuries of human experience are in themselves wrong and that their abolition will

53

necessarily lead men to the good and beautiful life, which is the only means whereby civilization can be saved.'

The memory of Reverend Mother Auxilia sitting in the parlour of her convent talking, with her white hands riding like doves on her lap, came to the colonel as he spoke and enabled him to talk with more conviction, because he thought that Reverend Mother Auxilia would understand even if Brigadier Catlock didn't.

'Reform by all means, but reform from within and not from without. Don't pull down the whole house because the mattress on your bed is uncomfortable. And don't imagine that the average sensual man is capable of governing himself, because he isn't. And if I thought that democracy meant being governed by the common lout, there'd be nothing for it but to follow the philosophy of Schopenhauer and go out and cut my throat with a razor in the bloody garden,' the colonel concluded.

The brigadier looked perplexed and slightly shocked until the telephone bell rang again and brought him back to the routine he understood.

'Catlock here,' he said. 'Yes, I did. Look here, Gascoyne-Savoy, what I wanted to say was this: I heard yesterday that one of your officers had been trying to see one of my officers and I want you to understand once and for all that this sort of thing has got to stop. Tell all your chaps from me that I insist on things being done through the proper channels. There are no "buts" about it: it's an order.' The brigadier replaced the receiver violently. 'This "old-boy basis" has gone far enough,' he said. 'Well, Hooky, what were we talking about?'

'Subversive activities, sir,' the colonel said. 'You were telling me that it was my job to put them down.'

'Of course, and you were talking some awful cock about righteousness,' the brigadier said, and yelped with laughter.

The colonel remembered having read in one of Aldous Huxley's books about the awful gulf that could yawn between two armchairs, and realized with dismay that a chasm and not a desk separated him from the brigadier, although they were both soldiers of King George, with all their red tabs on.

'Sorry, Hooky, if I hurt your feelings, but sometimes I think you're inclined to get just a little bit too theoretical, if you don't mind my saying so,' the brigadier said. 'Now let's get down to brass tacks.' The brigadier consulted some papers on his desk, blowing the words soundlessly on his lips as he read them over. 'Briefly, the term "subversive activities" means any act or propaganda contrary to the policy of His Majesty's Government or the policy of the Allies of His Majesty's Government.'

'And if the policy of any of the Allies of His Majesty's Government is itself contrary to the policy of His Majesty's Government, what then?' Colonel Nicobar asked.

'Look here, Hooky, what do you always want to go making things difficult for?' Brigadier Catlock said. 'All you've got to do is to use your loaf, although if things get really tricky I quite realize that you'll have to put them up to me for a decision.' Once again the telephone bell rang, and the brigadier reached for the receiver, cupping it eagerly to his ear. 'No, I was not at the Battle of Alamein, but I don't mind coming to the dinner if the booze is good, but for God's sake no Austrian gin,' he said.

This time the brigadier spoke for a greater length of time on the telephone and the colonel had time to reflect that he knew exactly what the brigadier was going to tell him about subversive activities. The brigadier was going to say that, as His Majesty's Government had backed Stalin and Tito and the Warsaw Government, every act or opinion contrary to the new totalitarianism at present in practice in these countries partook of the nature of subversive activity if not of treason and treachery. The colonel remembered what the brigadier had said in Rome when the news of Labour's victory in the British elections had first been announced: 'Don't worry, Hooky, old boy, somebody's got to make a nonsense of things and it had better be those chaps than us.' He also remembered what Lieutenant Catlock had said about Ramsay MacDonald in September, 1924, when Labour had got in for the first time: 'Of course the man's a cad, Hooky; he's a Socialist, isn't he?' And now the brigadier was more Marxist than his new masters, perhaps because he was surprised that they had allowed him to go on hanging on to the upper branches of the tree. The colonel found himself hoping that Mr. Ernest Bevin saw a little more clearly from the windows of the Foreign Office than his subordinates from the ground.

'Now, look here, Hooky; it's quite simple really,' the brigadier continued when he had finished his telephone conversation. 'All you've got to remember is this: all activities prejudicial to the Soviets and the new Poles and the Jugs have got to be stamped out. And of course the Austrians themselves have got to be watched: we can't risk any recrudescence of that Nazi business. Indeed, I have it from the highest level that H.M.G. would be most annoyed if the Austrians started any funny business of that sort.' The brigadier brought his revolving eyes to a standstill and succeeded in looking simultaneously both fleetingly wise and permanently threatening. 'And if I were you, Hooky, I'd keep my eyes on the Displaced Persons, who are up to all sorts of nefarious dodges, so they tell me.'

'But surely, sir, that is the job of the Displaced Persons Division,' Colonel Nicobar said.

'It's your job, Hooky, I tell you, and if you have any trouble with anybody trying to prevent you

57

doing your work properly, just let me know and I'll tear a few strips off him,' the brigadier said. 'In other words, in all matters regarding subversive activities you're the chap and you take orders from nobody except, of course, from me. Democratic dogma, Hooky, that's what you've got to defend.'

The colonel wasn't quite sure if he knew what democratic dogma meant, but he didn't like to ask the brigadier for a definition, partly because he didn't think that the brigadier knew either, partly because the brigadier was already talking on the telephone again, this time about whether sandwiches were to be served with drinks at quadripartite meetings; so he put on his hat, saluted and went out.

When he returned to his office, the colonel found the Rumanian general and his subordinates still looking for the sixty thousand loyal Rumanians who had fought on the side of the Allies, but they didn't seem to be looking very hard, because they were all listening to Audrey, who was sitting on top of her desk swinging her legs and talking world affairs.

'My dear general, I'm certain there's going to be another war, although I don't suppose so really,' she was telling the top of the general's monster hat, her face full of the confident emptiness of youth.

VI

WHEN SCHWESTER KASIMIRA peeled potatoes
she peeled them to the greater glory of God, just as
her holy mother Saint Walburga of Graz had done,
every snick of the knife a prayer and not always a
sad one either. Schwester Kasimira had become a
nun because once, when she was a very young girl,
her parents had taken her to the opera in Rome.
The opera was called *La Forza del Destino* and at the
beginning of the second act, which represented a
Spanish *fiesta*, the tenor had made the sign of the
cross and sung, 'In nomine Patris, et Filii, et Spiritus
Sancti' and then, when prayer was over, had raised
his glass and continued, 'Viva la buona compagnia.'
The thought had then occurred to her that, as it was
no longer easy to be prayerful in a world which had
divorced pleasure from God, there was only one
solution left and that was to be gay in a convent.
She had never told any of the other nuns about this,
because she knew that they all had their special
reasons for having become nuns and didn't speak
about them much, except Schwester Michaela of
Jesus Found Teaching in the Temple, who was always talking about the lovely dresses she had worn at
dances and how beautiful they had looked reflected

59

upside down on the polished floors of ballrooms, and of how that was why she had become a nun, because she had realised that pink taffeta was vanity.

Tonight, however, as she peeled, Schwester Kasimira was not feeling particularly gay, because she was trying to resist a temptation to a sin of carnal appetite: that of popping one of the potatoes into her mouth and swallowing it raw. She knew that the potato would never have been missed, because both the Herr Major McPhimister and the Fräulein Ober-Leutnant Quail were out to dine and the Herr Oberst was dining in alone and could not possibly eat all the potatoes that there were himself; but the potato was a British Army potato, and Schwester Kasimira knew that she had no right to eat British Army potatoes, even although she had agreed to help the cook for the mess. So she reminded herself that Jesus had probably felt very much hungrier when He had been fasting in the wilderness, and listened to the colonel singing upstairs in his bath, although she was afraid it wasn't a hymn he was singing, because the words 'mine's a gin, dearie,' kept coming in over and over again.

Schwester Kasimira rather liked the colonel, and the way his breath often smelled of trifle, which reminded her of when she had been a little girl. She never quite knew what to say to him, but she liked the way he smiled at her in the passage, with his face all crinkled up and kind-looking and his big red moustache which reminded her of her own father, who hadn't been a very holy man either, at least she had never thought so. But even if the colonel wasn't holy and never seemed to go to church, she was sure that he didn't think it silly of her to be a nun, like she sometimes thought the Herr Major McPhimister and Fräulein Quail did. Mother Auxilia seemed to like the colonel too, although she didn't seem to like his smelling of trifle so much, because once, when Schwester Kasimira had asked her whether she didn't think it nice, she had replied a little tartly, 'White Horse trifle, my dear,' and walked away with a reproving rattle of her rosary. Anyway, the colonel couldn't really be very wicked, even although he was a heretic, because otherwise Reverend Mother wouldn't have been so insistent about their all praying for his conversion in chapel. Which suggested to her that she might as well say a little extra prayer for his conversion now.

Even although she was a nun, Schwester Kasimira always found it difficult to say the Lord's Prayer bang right through without thinking of something else. Try as she would, she could never manage to mean every clause. Sometimes it would be the fervour of her intentions to mean every word she was praying which prevented her meaning them; at other times it would be familiarity with the words breeding spiritual sloth, of which she was very much ashamed, because she knew that not even the saints had been able to invent as good words themselves.

This time it was the image of the colonel himself which prevented her praying adequately for his conversion, for each time that she tried to say 'Hallowéd be Thy Name,' she didn't think of God's name being hallowed at all, but of how the colonel would look praying in chapel. This did not altogether surprise her, because she had always found it difficult to say the prayers of the rosary and at the same time meditate upon the mysteries, although she knew that Saint Dominic must have known how, because our Lady had revealed the devotion to him. After her fifth effort she succeeded both in articulating the petition and meaning it and was beginning to boggle over 'Thy Kingdom come,' when she looked up and found the colonel standing beside her and smiling, but not looking at all as though he were about to be converted, because he was holding a large glass filled with pale yellow drink in his hand.

'Guten Abend, Schwester Kasimira,' the colonel said. 'Always working, I see.'

'Il le faut bien, mon colonel,' Schwester Kasimira answered in French, because she knew that the colonel didn't really speak German, however fluently he might be beginning to be able to say 'Guten Abend.'

They both stood smiling foolishly at each other, neither knowing quite what to say. The nun saw a rugged tufty face of the sort which she had always been taught to believe was very worldly and the colonel saw a pair of timid brown eyes set deep above the pallid swell of colourless cheeks. Each, as they smiled, tried to convey the sympathy which they could not formulate in words, because each knew that the other's thoughts had been ruled by a different discipline, whose idiom was also different. Beyond his smile the colonel was trying to say that soldiers were not all as wicked as the nun might believe them to be; and behind her smile the nun was trying to think across to the colonel that holiness was not as dull as soldiers imagined and that it was courage and not cowardice which impelled people to forsake the world and walk with God. Each, of course, failed, but only in a measure, because the shyness of them both made them realise each other's sincerity, and their comprehension was aided by the beauty of the evening, slipping into night outside the window.

'I hope that neither my officers nor myself are being a bother to you,' the colonel said at length.

'Please believe, colonel, that it is a pleasure to have you here,' Schwester Kasimira said.

'It is kind of you so to interpret a necessity of war, sister,' the colonel said.

'But the war is over now, colonel, is it not?' Schwester Kasimira said.

'The war is over, sister, but the necessities of war continue,' the colonel said, and then understood that it would be foolish to attempt to explain to a nun the horrible new patterning-out of the world, with a new lump of threat rising as soon as one had levelled down the last.

For what could a nun, whose business was with eternity, understand about the correlation of history and of how he himself might not have been standing here talking to her today if Richelieu had been a different sort of priest and Karl Marx hadn't written his book? How otherwise could she interpret subversive activities than as sin against God, elderly lechers pouring champagne into satin dancing slippers? What could she understand about Brigadier Catlock and the policy of His Majesty's Government?

Then he caught sight of her hands, swollen and calloused and with black lines in the wrinkles and beneath her nails, and was suddenly humble and ashamed of having been on the winning side of the war when she had been on the losing. 'Here let me do that,' he said watching her damp knife gouging away at the potato.

'But, colonel,' Schwester Kasimira protested. 'And in any case Reverend Mother wouldn't like it.'

'You leave Reverend Mother to me,' the colonel said, taking both the knife and the potato from the nun and hoping that she wouldn't notice that he was trying to do with one hand what she had been doing with two. 'I'm a dab at dealing with Reverend Mothers; at least I think I am. After all Reverend Mothers can't be so very different from sergeants-major and it's more than twenty years now since I was last afraid of a sergeant-major. That's when an officer really begins to know that he is an officer: when he's no longer afraid of the sergeant-major.'

Observing from the gravity of her eyes that she did not understand his pleasantry, he tried to amuse her by talking his atrocious German. 'Ich kann auch die Kleider von den Kartoffeln abnehmen,' he said. 'Eplucher les pommes de terre, compris? And in any case it's my batman's job to help you.'

'But your batboy has gone out to the Kino,' Schwester Kasimira said.

The colonel laughed a lot at 'batboy,' and then, observing that she was still watching him with sad perplexity, asked her if she had had any relations fighting in the war.

'I had a brother who was a lieutenant-colonel in the German infantry,' she said. 'He was fighting in Russia and I have had no news of him since more than two years. If he is a prisoner I hope that he will come back, but if he is dead I hope that he died a good death, but I am a little afraid for him because he liked pleasure a lot, but perhaps God was kind to him at the end.' She looked at him with timid appeal. 'Please not to laugh at me,' she said. 'God must matter terribly to men when they are lying bleeding to death in the snow. The memory of the laughter of friends and the tinkle of glasses doesn't help them when one is alone for the last time in pain and with final knowledge of the purpose of life.'

'Please believe that I am very far from laughing at you, sister,' the colonel said, fumbling his potato in his emotion and letting it fall to the floor. 'Blast that bloody potato,' he nearly said, but checked himself in time and substituted a silent little meditation for the expletives which had nearly crossed his lips.

His thought was that he was sure that he would have liked Schwester Kasimira's brother if he had known him and have understood that he was not to be blamed for fighting on the side of the Nazis. Both in this war and in the last war he had always admired soldiers on the other side who fought with courage. Sometimes he had admired them so much that he had wondered why they had been fighting against one another and he had often thought of the tragedy of young faces upturned to the sky without their minds ever having quite known why the sacrifice had been demanded of them. For in the desert and in Italy one hadn't heard much talk of politics, about which the war was said to have been fought, and he didn't suppose things had been much different in the German Army, once the hurt had begun to tear men's bodies. Death, even of an enemy, had always distressed him and he was distressed for Schwester Kasimira now wondering about her brother behind her pale face. If only, he wished, all the decent chaps in the world could get together and kill all the dirty swine; but he didn't expect that solution would appeal to Schwester Kasimira, who would much prefer the decent chaps to pray for the dirty swine, in the hope that they would one day seek the Graal.

'But your poor arm, colonel,' Schwester Kasimira said, noticing for the first time the manipulation to which the colonel was forced in order to peel the potatoes with one hand. 'Forgive me, I had not realised.' She looked at him out of great pitying eyes, compassion lighting the pale ordinariness of her face to beauty. 'Forgive me too if I have said any-thing which I should not have said. You see, I do not know how soldiers feel about these things.'

'Soldiers do not feel at all about these things,' the colonel began to say, and then he realized that the statement was not quite true and that it would be unfair of him to attempt to win the nun's admiration by seeming to be braver than he was. 'At least, they learn not to feel about these things, because the loss of limbs becomes a habit like the loss of anything else. It's at the beginning that it hurts, when you think your loss is a tragedy.' He had nearly said '. . . when you wonder if the girls will like you any more,' but he had decided that the nun wouldn't under-stand that and that he wouldn't like her so much if she did.

Wondering what to say next, he remembered his last visit to Roehampton, to have repaired the artificial arm he rarely wore. There had been plenty of new young boys without arms and new young

67

boys without legs too, stumping about anonymously outside the headlines, and he had found it easier to feel sorrier for them than for himself. He had been flattered, too, by the readiness with which they had listened to him when he had dared to give them his outdated counsel and had hoped that the girls would be kind to them, too, and that the financial magnates would understand, behind their smooth, unsorrowing faces, that these wounds these boys had on Crispin's Day. 'One gets used to everything in the long run,' he said, wishing that he could think of something less trite.

'Perhaps that is the tragedy of things,' Schwester Kasimira said. 'One gets used even to sanctifying grace. What one really needs is a new little conversion every day, a fresh bright light inside oneself to make one anxious to light fresh bright lights in other people. Perhaps that's what our Lord meant when He said that there was more joy in heaven over one sinner that repenteth than about all those who keep His commandments. Perhaps that's why the workers who come into the vineyard at the eleventh hour are paid the same wages as those who have borne the heat and burden of the day: because they have enthusiasm in their souls.' A breeze came in at the window and caught her veil, flapping it momentarily into a black sail billowing behind her earnest face. 'But perhaps it is a little difficult for you to understand what I am saying,' she said.

The colonel liked the way the nun said 'Our Lord.' The tone in which she said it made him wonder if the secular manner of his life during the last thirty years were the sanity he had imagined it to be. Only yesterday afternoon he had heard Brigadier Catlock bawling over the telephone: 'For Christ's sake, Bill, old boy, you've got to stay and help me give these Unrra bitches afternoon tea.' He wondered what sort of look would have come into Schwester Kasimira's eyes if she had heard a remark like that. Probably she would have prayed for a fortnight over it. Looking at her now, he almost felt like praying for a fortnight over it himself.

'I think I understand,' he said. 'It's like that in the Army too. Some days one feels proud of being a soldier: you know, serving an ideal and that sort of thing. And then one comes up against the grocers in uniform, the chaps who are trying to blow themselves up into brigadiers and major-generals, and then one is not so proud.' He stopped as he realised that there was no real parallel in what he had been saying. 'Put it another way,' he said. 'I try to be decent.'

'I am sure that you do and I shall pray a lot for you,' Schwester Kasimira said. 'That is another trouble with the world today. Not only do people not try: they do not even try to try and that is where real sinfulness comes in.'

The colonel knew that the nun had hit the nail on the head once again. The couldn't-t-care-less boys, the chaps who imagined that now that the war was over there was no need for further effort, the soldiers that slopped past officers without saluting, the Very Important Persons who talked eloquent tripe with their lips and dissembled in their fatty hearts, the morons and the knaves who played for the present rather than for the future, the cacklers at parties and the delighters in horses' legs, they weren't trying to try because they thought that nobody else was trying to try either. It was, of course, a contagion from which the world had always suffered, but it was much more dangerous now than in the time of Charles the Second, when boys of nineteen had not been able to destroy cathedrals by pressing buttons. The peace of the evening outside plastered against the window was an illusion. Disaster threatened the world unless a prophet arose. For a brief moment he almost decided to become the prophet himself and in the urgency of his emotion let another potato fall to the floor.

'I really must insist on doing my own work,' the nun said. 'You'll cut yourself if you aren't careful.'

'If I give in will you dine with me?' the colonel said, both because he felt lonely and thought it would do Schwester Kasimira good to eat some decent food for once. 'Perhaps Reverend Mother would come too. And we could ask Schwester Michaela as well. After all, the others are out and there's plenty of food.'

'That is a very kind thought, but I am afraid that
I must refuse,' the nun said, deliberately taking the
knife away from him. 'You see, I do not think that
our Holy Founder, Saint Walburga of Graz, would
approve. She was a very holy woman,' she went
on to explain, observing the colonel's incompre-
hension. 'One of her rules is that her spiritual
daughters must on no account nourish themselves in
the company of those who are not members of the
community, unless they are other female religious
visiting one of our houses. It was a rule which she
herself kept when she flew to Rome in 1585 to inform Pope Sixtus the Fifth that in her opinion only
drastic internal reform of the Church could prevent
further schism in Europe. The Pope invited her to
take a collation with him, but she insisted that as
there were no other members of her community at
the Vatican she would have to eat alone.'

'Flew to Rome?' the colonel asked. 'In 1585?'

'Our Holy Founder was borne through the air on
the wings of an angel,' Schwester Kasimira explained simply. 'That was one of the miracles
authenticated at her canonization in 1707. There
were others, of course. For instance, so great was the
presence of the Holy Ghost within her, and with so
great ebullition did it fill her, that she was frequently
raised from the ground during the celebration of
Mass. This occurred most often when she knelt at
the altar rails to receive Holy Communion, so that

71

on several occasions the celebrant had to climb up a ladder in order to be able to lay the Sacred Host on her tongue.'

'I can see perfectly well that the colonel does not believe in the possibility of miracles.' Looking round, Schwester Kasimira and the colonel saw that Reverend Mother Auxilia had entered the pantry and was standing behind them with her hands folded beneath her scapular, balanced on the big bump of the skirt of her ample black habit. For Reverend Mother had no legs and she didn't need them, and her Holy Founder, Saint Walburga of Graz, hadn't had any legs either as had been clearly perceived in 1583, 1584, and 1587 by the members of her community, who had seen her levitated during her devotions. 'The Herr Oberst obviously belongs to that school of thought which denies that the Creator has any power over His own creation and imagines that any manifestations of His power must take place within the limits of the laws which He Himself created.'

'I am afraid, Reverend Mother, that you do me an injustice,' the colonel said. 'As a matter of fact, I belong to no school of thought at all.'

'That, Herr Oberst, is precisely as I had imagined,' Reverend Mother said.

After that there was nothing left for the colonel to do but to take up his unfinished whisky-and-soda and slink, guiltily, out of the pantry.

VII

I'M AFRAID Twingo's made a muddle and it's
Jugoslav Volksdeutsche and not Rumanian Volksdeutsche he ought to have said, though, as far as I
and the colonel can make out, there's no evidence of
their indulging in subversive activities of any sort,'
Audrey was saying over the telephone, with a nylon
knee almost jammed down the mouthpiece. 'Why,
I'd love to. The Park at seven. In the bar. Of
course, I remember you perfectly. That's right. A
Volksdeutscher's not the same as a Reichsdeutscher,
although I don't know exactly where the difference
comes in, although I believe it's fearfully political,
really. Of course I'll wear my black dress.'

Seated at his desk, the colonel was doing his best
not to listen. Subversive activities were at a standstill for the moment and the colonel was reading a
letter which had just arrived from his younger
daughter, who was fifteen: 'On Sunday afternoon I
went to the Fun Fair and went on the roundabouts
three times and the bumper cars twice. I also ate
five ice creams. Then I had tea when I ate a large
liver sausage sandwich which was good. Three of
the ice creams which I had were covered with chocolate on the outside. They were lovely. Miss Parkin-

73

son wonders if I'll be able to spend a holiday in Austria sometime, as she doesn't think my German will be good enough to get into the University unless I go to Austria first. The weather here is frightfully cold. I shiver in my winter frock and blazer . . .'

The colonel looked across at Audrey and wondered if she had ever written letters like Sarah. Probably she had, only ten years ago, in 1935, when Mussolini and Ciano had been talking big. The realisation of her youth made him feel temporarily tolerant of her. What should they know of Volksdeutsche who only Volksdeutsche knew? Perhaps in ten years' time Sarah would be bawling with authoritative inaccuracy down a telephone about the Kremlin.

Sergeant Moonlight came in with a letter flagged: 'MOST IMMEDIATE.' The letter read: 'The Director of Investigations into Subversive Activities will prepare for Brigadier C. M. V. Catlock, D.S.O., M.C., by 0900 hrs on 17th August a brief on "The Strategical Aspects of Communism."'

'That's an easy one, sir,' Sergeant Moonlight said, observing the colonel's frown. 'It says in all the newspapers that communism has become rampart; I suppose that means there's no getting over it, sir.'

'Send me a typist at once, Moonlight,' the colonel said.

'There ain't no typists, sir,' Sergeant Moonlight said. 'Jemima's gone out to ave a cup of tea . . .'

'Jemima?' the colonel said.

'Private Brownlee, I mean, sir; and Jane — Private Jenkins, I mean, sir — as gone to ave a bath,' Sergeant Moonlight said.

'Then get me another typist,' the colonel said.

'There ain't no other typists, sir,' Sergeant Moonlight said. 'The war establishment only provides for two, sir.'

'The war establishment has no business only to provide for two typists,' the colonel said.

'I'm afraid that ain't my can, sir; that's the brigadier's can,' Sergeant Moonlight said.

'I can see I shall have to talk seriously to Twingo,' the colonel said. 'He ought to know better than to allow both typists out of the office at once.'

'Perhaps I can help, sir,' Audrey said. 'I don't do shorthand exactly, but I can do quick squiggles.'

'All right, then, let's try the quick squiggles,' the colonel said. He waited until Audrey had fluttered her notebook, her knees and her eyelashes into position, and then began: 'Brief for Brigadier C. M. V. Catlock, D.S.O., M.C., on the Strategical Aspects of Communism full stop. Although in Soviet Russia communism has long ceased to preach the apostolic doctrine of equality comma in central and southwestern Europe its agents fan the discontent of the undernourished masses by informing them that they have the right to live as grandly as their masters who have exploited them full stop.'

'It's all right, sir, you don't need to dictate the

punctuation,' Audrey said. 'After all, I read *John O' London's Weekly*.'

'To this argument the mechanic responds more eagerly than the peasant comma who comma illiterate though he may be comma,' the colonel was continuing with emphasis, when the door of his office opened and Colonel Omicron entered, with the customary concentration of disciplined stupidity shining eagerly from his eyes.

'Hooky, you old scoundrel,' he greeted.

'Blinker,' the colonel said despondently.

'How funny, I had a dream about you only last night, although there was a wing commander in my dream as well, but really it was chiefly about you — it just shows you there must be something in dreams after all, doesn't it?' Audrey said, rippling under her blouse and skirt.

'I've dreamt about you, too, my dear,' Colonel Omicron said, beginning to look devout, until he realised that Colonel Nicobar was watching him. 'Smatter of fact, I didn't see that cad in Padua after all, so I've come up to see another cad about another job here and in the meantime . . .'

'And in the meantime you were wondering if I would allow you to take Senior Subaltern Quail out to tea,' Colonel Nicobar said.

'Hooky, you're a wonder,' Colonel Omicron said. 'Easy seen he's been through Staff College, isn't it, Miss Quail?'

'Now look here, Blinker, we're frightfully pleased to see you, of course, but both Miss Quail and I are busy,' Colonel Nicobar said. 'We're doing a brief for the brigadier on communism.'

'Communism, that's easy,' Colonel Omicron said. 'You just tell him from me that communism's all my eye and Betty Martin, and if he doesn't like that to go and stick communism on the wall. We've answered that one, haven't we, Miss Quail, and now what about a dish of tea?'

'May I, sir?' Audrey asked demurely. Already she was stroking her hair, streaking her eyebrows, smearing her lips. 'Private Brownlee is sure to be back by now, anyway.'

Private Brownlee was back, and, when Colonel Omicron and Audrey had gone out, she came in, sat down and poised her pencil, and mooned out through the open window.

'Brief for Brigadier C. M. V. Catlock, D.S.O., M.C., on the Strategical Aspects of Communism,' the colonel began. 'Although in Soviet Russia communism has long ceased to preach the apostolic doctrine of equality, in central and southwestern Europe its agents fan the discontent of the under-nourished masses by informing them that they have the right to live as grandly as their masters who have exploited them. To this argument the mechanic responds more eagerly than the peasant, who, illiterate though he may be . . .'

'Please, sir, where do I put the doo-dahs?' the typist asked.

'Don't *you* read *John O' London's Weekly*, then?' the colonel asked.

'Never eard of it, sir. Is it a paper like?'

But before the colonel could tell her about *John O' London's Weekly* or where to put the doo-dahs, the telephone rang, with Brigadier Catlock at the other end, wanting to see him immediately.

'Sorry, Hooky, but the general has sent for me,' Brigadier Catlock informed the colonel as soon as he arrived. 'However, Gideon will tell you exactly what I want, won't you, Gideon?' He nodded in the direction of a smaller desk, at which a young man with a swarthy, insolent, lineless face was reading a copy of the *Tatler*. 'And don't forget about that new wallpaper for my bedroom, will you, Giddy?'

Captain Gideon started off by calling the colonel 'sir,' but he used the vocative in such a way as to make it clear that he didn't think he ought to be calling the colonel 'sir' at all, since he was related to a lord who owned all the preference shares in Gideon's Glamour Perfumes, Limited, and had himself composed the text of the advertisement which read: 'Don't Kill Romance by Stinking at the Dance: Deal B.O. a K.O.'

'This is the way it is, sir,' he said. 'The brigadier wants a brief on subversive activities, their past, their present, and their future. I think you had better start off by defining the term "subversive activities" and then go on and set out the historical perspective with special reference to Austria, of course, and end up with the picture as it is today and what it is likely to be six months hence, again with special reference to Austria.'

'Look here, you young lout,' the colonel nearly said, but didn't, because he knew that Gideon would make the most of it afterwards when telling the brigadier. 'Look here, Gideon,' he said instead, 'as the brigadier himself informed me only a few days ago of the precise nature of subversive activities, I can't quite see why he wants me to inform him about them now. And in any case I've already got a brief to write for him on communism.'

'You can't expect the brigadier to remember everything he says,' Captain Gideon said coldly. 'After all, he informs so many people about so many subjects. And the communism brief still stands, of course.'

'What I should like to know is how the brigadier expects me to do my work if I'm continually being forced to write reports about it,' the colonel said.

'I'm afraid that's a question which you must ask the brigadier personally,' Captain Gideon said. 'And there's one other thing, sir: the Soviets have asked us to locate a girl called Maria Bühlen who is wanted by them. It appears that she is a very fine ballet dancer who left Russia before the beginning

79

of the war because she did not agree with the communist ideology. During the war she danced in Vienna, although there is no suggestion that the expression of her art was carried out for any purpose other than that of earning her livelihood.'

'Bühlen, surely that is a German name?' the colonel said.

'The Soviets have informed us that she is to be regarded as a Soviet citizen and the brigadier has ruled that we are to accept their interpretation,' Captain Gideon said, with one eye on a page of photographs of a hunt ball, at which a crowd of Englishmen closely resembling himself had been photographed drinking champagne while they weren't thinking about the spiritual issues of the war.

When he got back to his office, the colonel found three signals from the War Office in his in-tray. The first read: 'Request immediate information on the organization in Austria of the Sicherheitspolizei'; the second read: 'Request immediately numbers of married officers belonging to Vlassov's Cossacks, together with numbers of children under twelve repeat twelve'; the third read: 'Furnish before nine hundred hours tomorrow details of anti-Tito publications appearing clandestinely in Austria.'

Audrey was still out having a dish of tea with Colonel Omicron, but Private Brownlee had placed a draft of the beginning of the colonel's brief on communism on his desk; it read:

'Brief for Brigadier C. M. V. Catlock dsomc on the strategical aspects of communism although in Soviet Russia communism has long ceased to preach the carbolic doctrine of quality in central and south-western europe its agents fan the discontent of the masses by informing them that they have the right to live as grandly as their pastors who have expected them to this argument the machinery responds more eagerly than the pheasant who illegitimate though he may be . . .'

'I might as well own up and admit that I didn't get it right all by myself, sir,' Private Brownlee said when she came in to take the remainder of the dictation. 'Jane gave me an and; she's ad er bath now, sir.'

VIII

Audrey was out dining with the pop-eyed brigadier and Twingo was out, too, trying out a new girl from England, so once again the colonel had dinner alone, and now he was reading a novel which Sergeant Moonlight had lent him that morning called *One Glorious Week in Paris*. 'Red ot, sir,' Sergeant Moonlight had said, and the colonel had taken him at his word, because he was tired and wanted to be amused. Reverend Mother Auxilia came into the room unexpectedly while he was reading it and the colonel had difficulty in sliding the book, with his one hand, down the back of the chair in which he was sitting without Reverend Mother seeing.

'Herr Oberst, I should be very grateful if you could afford me a few minutes of your time,' she said. 'I have a very important request to make of you, and if you do not mind, I should prefer to make it in my own room.'

Reverend Mother Auxilia's room was much less austere than the colonel had imagined that it would be. There were curtains and there were books with gold lettering at the back of the covers and on the mantelpiece there was a photograph of two small girls in old-fashioned party frocks.

'My sister and myself,' Reverend Mother explained. 'Perhaps you will be able to say which of them is me.'

The colonel took up the frame and looked into the faded photograph. Both of the small girls were chubby and jolly and neither of them looked as though she would ever become a nun.

'That one,' the colonel said at length.

'Wrong; I am the other,' Reverend Mother said. 'I do not blame you for not recognizing me: I am much more bad-tempered now.'

'Experience of the world makes us all bad-tempered in the long run, Reverend Mother,' the colonel said.

Through the open window the colonel could see that there were lights in the chapel. With the trees growing all round it was difficult to make out which were branches and which were saints' robes on stained glass. In the chapel the nuns were praying that the Lord would give peace in their time, although they were beginning to be afraid that He wouldn't.

'Sometimes I think that you are a bit of a butterfly, Herr Oberst,' Reverend Mother said.

'Perhaps you are right, Reverend Mother,' the colonel said, laughing at her use of the term. 'My brothers all turned out much better than I did. One's a colonial bishop in the Anglican Church and the other's a successful banker in New York.' He thought for a few seconds about his brothers and decided that he didn't care if he never saw either of them again.

'Anyway, even if you are the black horse of your family, I am thinking that I can trust you,' Reverend Mother Auxilia said. 'Herr Oberst, I want to ask your advice. Before you came here we had Russian officers billeted in this convent. At first they were rough and mocking, but gradually they came to see that our way of life was not intended to harm them and they stopped laughing at us because we were believing in God. And then, when they went away and before you were coming, a girl came to us in great trouble and said that the Russians were looking for her and wanted to send her back to Russia because they were thinking that she had been a traitor to Russia during the war. The girl's name is Maria Bühlen.'

'Go on, Reverend Mother,' the colonel said.

'She asked us to give her shelter and I agreed,' Reverend Mother Auxilia continued. 'To begin with, she is a Catholic, and although she is perhaps too beautiful to find it very easy to be holy, she is very devout at Mass and prays a lot in the chapel alone, but perhaps that is because she is in trouble. When the people in the world learn to pray also when they are glad and gay, Herr Oberst, perhaps then they will have no need of foreign ministers to talk to other foreign ministers about international

84

security. But I am digressing. The girl is not really a Russian, but a German, as her parents were members of the German colony in Russia known as the Volga Germans. When she was very young, she went to Moscow and learned to be a dancer in the ballet and became a prima ballerina. But when war broke out between Germany and Russia and all the Volga colony of Germans were deported to Siberia, she fled, and eventually after many trials came to Austria, where she was foolish enough to dance in Vienna. The Russians want her back very badly and sooner or later I am afraid that they will be thinking of looking for her here. I cannot turn her away, because of what our Lord said in the gospels, and yet I am frightened about what will happen to my nuns if the Russians find her here, because they will be very angry. And also I am a little frightened for you, Herr Oberst, because you are the ally of the Russians, and they may think that you are having some share in her concealment.'

The colonel was thinking out just what he was going to say to Reverend Mother Auxilia when Schwester Kasimira came in with her face much whiter than usual and said that two Russian officers with a squad of Russian soldiers were downstairs, demanding to search the house.

As he followed Reverend Mother and Schwester Kasimira downstairs, Colonel Nicobar tried to think

out what course of action it was his duty to take in
view of the conflicting loyalties between which he
was placed, God or mammon, Reverend Mother
Auxilia or Brigadier Catlock, and which, for a
Protestant serving soldier, of the latter two was
Mammon? 'Always say "yes" when you get an
order and say "yes" like hell and use your common
sense when you get an order you can't obey,' old
Tweezer had once said to him during the last war,
when they had been lying out in a shell-hole watching troops being torn to shreds, because the staff
officers at Corps H.Q. had got hold of the wrong
maps by mistake. Old Tweezer was a lieutenant-
general now, issuing orders like blue turpentine in
Baluchistan. Colonel Nicobar was still hoping that
they were the right orders when he reached the bottom of the staircase and found that Twingo had already come home and was talking to the Russian
officers at the top of his voice in Outer Hebridean
French.

'Ici une église, pas un théâtre,' he was saying,
'Religieuses, pas de cancan.'

There were two officers and six men. Both of the
officers wore tightly buttoned dark khaki tunics with
high collars and navy-blue baggy breeches with thin
red stripes down the sides and shiny black leggings.
One of the officers had gold epaulettes with two red
stripes running vertically down the middle and three
red stars and was obviously a full colonel; the other

had gold epaulettes with one red stripe and one red star and was a second lieutenant. The six men also wore dark khaki tunics and navy-blue baggy breeches, but of coarser material. On Colonel Nicobar's arrival the second lieutenant detached himself from the group, approached the colonel and saluted him.

'The colonel greets you,' he said in English. 'He hopes that you are indeed in excellent health.'

'Please thank the colonel for me and say that I am in excellent health and that I hope that he, too, is exceedingly healthy.'

The second lieutenant translated Colonel Nicobar's greeting to the Russian colonel who stood looking at Colonel Nicobar with tired sad pale grey eyes and then said a few sentences in rapid Russian.

'Colonel Piniev thanks the colonel for his kind wishes and asks the colonel if he is officially billeted in this convent,' the Russian second lieutenant translated.

'Tell him that his surmise is correct,' Colonel Nicobar said.

The Russian colonel looked surprised when Colonel Nicobar's remark had been translated to him.

'Colonel Piniev does not understand how the colonel's sunrise can be more correct than his own sunrise, since the sunrise is a phenomenon common to the whole world alike and is not more accurate in one country than another,' the Russian second lieutenant re-translated back. 'In any case, without in the least wishing to hurt the colonel's feelings, he does not quite clearly understand what the sunrise has to do with the matter in question.'

'Surmise not sunrise,' Colonel Nicobar said. 'Nicht die Sonne aber was der Herr Russische Oberst verstanden hat, das ist was richtig ist. Pas le lever du soleil,' he said in one last linguistic effort, addressing himself directly to the Russian colonel.

'English very difficult language,' the Russian colonel said. His tired face was lit with a brief beauty as he smiled and the two nuns and Colonel Nicobar and Twingo smiled too, glad to find a common ground for merriment, however momentary. For a few seconds Stalin, Pope Pius the Twelfth, and King George the Sixth laughed together in the persons of their representatives. Then the business which had brought them together was upon them once more, and their faces were grave again.

'In that case, if the colonel is living in this convent, it is to him that I must address myself as to the ally of Soviet Russia,' the Russian colonel said himself in surprisingly good English. 'We are believing that a young woman by the name of Maria Bühlen is in this convent. This young woman is a citizen of Soviet Russia and we are demanding her to be handed over to us in order that she may be sent home.'

'I have already been informed officially about the

case of this young woman,' Colonel Nicobar said. Out of the corner of his eye he remarked the surprise on Reverend Mother's face when he said this, but he did not dare to look at her openly, in case the Russian colonel should observe her attempting to communicate with him.

'In that case the colonel will be comprehending why this young woman must be handed over to us,' the Russian colonel continued. 'She is a citizen of Soviet Russia. It is illegal to reside abroad without official permission. Also she is being under suspicion of having spoken doctrines against the Soviet State. Also it is the right of the Soviet authorities to repatriate all Soviet citizens from the city of Vienna.'

'I understand perfectly,' Colonel Nicobar said.

'Then the colonel will also be understanding that I must be asking the Reverend Mother to hand over the young woman to me if she is in the building,' the Russian colonel went on. 'My right is also because her convent is in the Innerestadt which is ruled by the four Occupying Powers.'

Colonel Nicobar repeated all this to Reverend Mother Auxilia in bad French and worse German, although he knew that she had already understood what the Russian colonel had said in English. He did so because he was sure that she, like himself, required time to think. While he boggled over French subjunctives and German genders, he felt grateful to the Russian colonel for not having asked

Reverend Mother to state whether or not the girl
Maria Bühlen was living in the convent and so
having forced her to choose between telling a lie
and abandoning her protégé.

Reverend Mother Auxilia, however, appeared to
require no time to think.

'Tell the Herr Russische Oberst that I shall be
only too pleased if he will have my convent searched
by his men,' she said.

The Russian colonel gave orders to the Russian
second lieutenant who moved off up the stairs followed by the Russian soldiers, clumping after him.
Schwester Kasimira made as though to accompany
them, but the Russian colonel said '*Nyet*' sharply
and indicated to her that she was to remain where
she was; so they all stood about looking official, while
the Russian second lieutenant and his men marched
about heavily through the rooms above. Colonel
Nicobar had had for many years a theory about
people looking official and had concluded that men
looked official outside only on occasions when they
found it difficult to feel official inside. Behind the
Russian colonel's mask of tired impartiality and desire for justice he imagined that he could detect a
feeling of sympathy for Reverend Mother Auxilia
as behind the man with grey hair on his temples he
thought he could see the ghost of the boy who had
fished for minnows in Russian rivers, untroubled by
what Marx had thought about economics; even

Reverend Mother's pouchy expression of impersonal disapproval did not ring altogether true, although perhaps religious people found it easier than other people did to feel official, since they were more accustomed to disciplining their emotions.

The Russian second lieutenant and his men came back about ten minutes later. It was impossible to tell from the soldiers' faces what they were thinking.

The second lieutenant shot out a quick spate of syllables at the Russian colonel, who spoke in English to Colonel Nicobar.

'I am very sorry to have troubled you,' he said. 'It would appear that the young lady is not here. I should be liking, however, to see the nuns before we leave.'

Reverend Mother Auxilia bowed.

'My nuns are praying in the chapel, but if the Herr Oberst wishes I shall assemble them here,' she said.

'I am preferring to see them where they are,' the Russian colonel said.

This time the second lieutenant stayed with them in the hall and Colonel Piniev marched away with his men who didn't pray to inspect women who did. Darting a quick glance at Reverend Mother Auxilia, Colonel Nicobar imagined that he detected a slightly anxious expression on her face, but he didn't dare to look at her for long, in case the second lieutenant should be watching. Schwester Kasimira stood fingering the beads on her rosary, but as her lips didn't appear to be moving, the colonel didn't think that she was praying. The footsteps of the Russian soldiers clacked away down the stone passage and diminished into a silence which lasted for about five minutes. Then the soldiers came clacking back again, with the colonel at their heels.

'Once more I am apologizing,' the Russian colonel said.

'Please allow me to accompany you to the door,' Colonel Nicobar said. He remembered having read that the Soviets appreciated military compliments and he was more than willing to be courteous in the interests of international understanding.

When the Russian colonel had saluted the two nuns and the two nuns had bowed back to the Russian colonel, Colonel Nicobar walked with Colonel Piniev. The second lieutenant and the soldiers marched away down beneath the trees and the two colonels followed behind. Because they did not know what to say to each other, they moved along the path in silence, with the stars shining down through the leaves in pale gleams of brittle light. At the gateway they both stopped and stood smiling at each other with uncertainty. The second lieutenant and his men marched away down the road and the two colonels were alone with the darkness all about them. A fifteen hundredweight lurched by and the headlamps made lovely blurs on the leaves as they moved along the trees. Was all beauty insignificant, Colonel Nicobar wondered, a permutation of shadow or colour thrown by chance on a screen? The lines on the Russian colonel's tired face reassured him and made him hope. The noise o the lorry died away and the night became quiet again beneath the patience of the sky.

'Schöne Nacht,' Colonel Nicobar said. 'Belle soirée.'

'Very beautiful,' the Russian colonel said. 'Pretty stars.'

'English all think Stalin a great man,' Colonel Nicobar said.

'Churchill big man too. Smoke big cigar,' the Russian colonel said

'Only hope for world Stalin, Churchill, and Truman smoke three big cigars together,' Colonel Nicobar said.

'Stalin wants peace,' the Russian colonel said. 'Not just peace for Russia, but peace for the world. That why Stalin wants Maria Bühlen to be coming back to Russia. She is a great dancer. Sehr schön. She is a Volksdeutscher, but a Russian Volksdeutscher. If she will be dancing for Russia, she will have nothing to fear and all will be forgiven.'

'I think that I understand,' Colonel Nicobar said.

'Auf wiedersehen, Herr Oberst,' the Russian colonel said.

'Auf wiedersehen, Herr Oberst,' Colonel Nicobar said.

Back in the hall of the convent the colonel found Reverend Mother Auxilia, Schwester Kasimira, and Twingo all talking excitedly. They stopped as he entered.

'Just fancy, sir, she was here all the time,' Twingo said. 'Upon my word, Reverend Mother, I've never seen a better example of a poker face in all my life. And they say she's beautiful, too, sir. I'm ready to bet she's the girl I saw that first night in the chapel and that Reverend Mother's never allowed me to set eyes on since.'

'You'll see her yourself in a few minutes,' Reverend Mother said, making a sign to Schwester Kasimira, who departed immediately with swift noiselessness. 'I hope, Herr Oberst, that you did not think that I did wrongly in concealing her presence from the Russians. I know that I acted a lie even if I did not tell one, but it was a lie which was acted from motives of mercy and for which I think I shall be pardoned.'

'The end justifies the means, does it?' the colonel nearly said, but realized in time that it would be both unkind and unjust, because there was so obviously nothing calculating about Reverend Mother's countenance, with its serene look of worry about supernatural values. Instead, while they were waiting, he thought about how he was going to persuade Reverend Mother to let the girl go back to Russia, because it was quite clear that she must be repatriated, however much she didn't want to be, because

94

the Russian colonel had spoken in such evident good
faith and it was foolish to start off a peace on mis-
trust. Besides, he had his orders from Brigadier Catlock, who presumably had his from a yet higher level,
whose decisions were infallible, so, in spite of occa-
sional discouragement, he had never ceased to hope.
Care would, of course, have to be taken to arrange
the girl's repatriation in such a way that the Russians
would not discover that she had, in fact, been con-
cealed by the nuns in the convent.

It was then that the girl herself came in, led by
Schwester Kasimira, who was holding her hand.
She had fair hair and high cheekbones and deep
grave blue eyes. She was wearing a black silk frock
and her breasts were high in the bodice. Her legs
were long and thin and she moved with grace,
tumbling the lip of her dress as she walked.

'This is our little Maria Bühlen,' Reverend Mother
said. 'She is as good as she is pretty and we are very
glad to have her with us.'

'She must be good, or otherwise she would not
have looked so holy when dressed as a nun in
Schwester Michaela's old habit,' Schwester Kasimira
said. 'She was with us praying in chapel when the
Russian soldiers came and when the soldiers bent
to look into her face they drew away again immediately because she looked so holy.'

'I say, that was plucky of you,' Twingo said.

The girl did not answer, but stood smiling with

95

serene eyes. Watching her, the colonel could understand how the Russians had taken her for a nun, with her still face.

'But now you are safe and the Russians will not come back again here to look for you, so now you will no longer need to dress as a nun, although you will still require to be good, because that is God's will, that we should all be saints,' Schwester Kasimira said.

'Fräulein Bühlen must be very exhausted after all this excitement and I was wondering if she wouldn't care to come along with me to Sacher's for a drink,' Twingo said, alight with love.

The colonel decided that it was time to make himself unpopular.

'I am afraid that Fräulein Bühlen is not going to leave this convent until she comes with me to my office tomorrow morning,' he said. 'Reverend Mother, when you first informed me you were hiding this girl here, I had not time to tell you that I had received orders from my brigadier to hand her over to the Russians immediately; I had not time to tell you, because the Russians themselves arrived, and I could not tell you later, because I did not wish to give you away. I shall not betray you now, because I shall myself hand the girl over to the Russians without involving you in any way, but the girl must go back to Russia. If she had anything to fear I might hesitate; but I know that she has nothing to fear. I have the word of Colonel Piniev that she has nothing to fear. On the contrary, a great welcome awaits her, because the Russians are always ready to pardon artists, especially for crimes of which they have not been guilty. Fräulein, Sie haben nichts zu fürchten, absolument rien à craindre,' he concluded.

'Aber ich bin nicht Russe, ich bin Volksdeutsche,' the girl said. 'Meine Eltern auch Volksdeutsche und presto subito Siberia wo sie gestorben sind.'

'Sir, you can't do a thing like that; really you can't,' Twingo said.

'Herr Oberst, the girl is a good Catholic; you can't send a good Catholic back to a heathen land like Russia,' Reverend Mother Auxilia said.

'Perhaps it is the duty of a good Catholic to go to a heathen land like Russia,' the colonel said, trying not to look too much at any of them and least of all at Schwester Kasimira, with her big sad lustreless eyes. 'Perhaps it is the duty of the West to attempt to make the East trust it by itself trusting the East. At any rate, these are my orders, and you, Major McPhimister, will be responsible for seeing to it that Fräulein Bühlen does not leave this convent tonight and is brought to me in my office at nine hundred hours sharp tomorrow morning.'

He walked away without waiting for anyone to answer him and went up to his bedroom, where he closed the door and tried to go on believing that he had done the right thing.

IX

Colonel Omicron had found another cad to give him a job in Vienna, and tonight he was taking Audrey out to dine at the Kinsky Palace, which had just been opened as an Officers' Club, although it wasn't permitted to take Austrian girls there, no matter how beautiful they might be. Audrey, however, was as beautiful as any Austrian girl, and in her black taffeta she looked even more so, sailing round the Ring in an eight hundred weight Chevrolet known as a buzz-wagon which Colonel Omicron had managed to borrow from a friend who was away in Italy for the week-end, buying wine for a senior officers' mess.

The buzz-wagon made such a noise as it rootled down the road, narrowly avoiding collision with Russian lorries and Viennese trams, that it was impossible for either of them to hear what the other was saying, although Colonel Omicron had made an attempt to start a conversation going on highbrow level, by asking Audrey if she thought that Mr. Ernest Bevin was a good secretary of state for foreign affairs. When, however, he had shouted the question three times without obtaining any reply other than a shaking of Audrey's silky black hair and a blank smile, he abandoned the endeavour and did not speak again until they reached Sacher's Hotel, where they were to begin the evening by having a drink in the bar.

The bar was crammed with horsey-looking young men with mammoth moustaches who had come up from the British Zone of Austria to Vienna for the week-end. They all switched round on their stools when Audrey and the colonel entered, staring in what Colonel Omicron considered was a most offensive manner. That was the trouble with the young fellows these days, the colonel reflected, as he steered Audrey past the concupiscent gaze of a captain in the Royal Irish Fusiliers, they had no savoir-faire. Probably that was why young girls like Audrey preferred to go out with men of his own age, who didn't rush at things like a bull at a gate, but practised dalliance with dignity and understood that love-making was none the less attractive for being flavoured with a touch of culture.

Audrey sat down, arranged the flow of her frock over her knees and looked over the occupants of the room with a critical eye.

'Eighth Army's going down the drain now that it's become B.T.A.' she said. 'British Troops in Austria. Did you ever hear of such a silly name! I told the Field Marshal that it was a mistake to change an historic name, but of course, with

Twenty-One Army Group becoming B.A.O.R., I
said that I quite understood his point about Austria
having to come into line with Germany, although
if Tito started a nonsense over Carinthia I told him
quite plainly that I couldn't guarantee what the out-
come would be.'

Colonel Omicron purred beneath the bright buttons of his tunic. He had always suspected that the
girl was intelligent and now she was proving it. That
was what those young supercilious oafs at the bar
didn't understand: that just because a girl was pretty,
it didn't mean that she wasn't interested in intellec-
tual subjects like politics. And even if she weren't
interested in politics, that didn't mean that she liked
the do-you-play-tennis — do-you-play-golf silly-ass
sort of approach. Technique, that was what the
young chaps lacked, the ability to win a girl's affection by appealing first of all to her intellect. Sure of
his ground, the colonel scowled threateningly at two
young majors opposite who were staring at Audrey
with insistence. Then he called the waiter over and
Audrey had an opportunity of airing her Italian,
because the waiter had once worked in Perugia.

'Io voglio . . .' she began.

'Un martini,' Colonel Omicron suggested, who
also spoke the language fluently, when he wasn't in
Italy.

'Shut up like a dear, will you, Blinker,' Audrey
said. 'You ought to know me well enough by now to

realise that I never can talk Italian well when other people are talking it badly.' She beamed at the waiter with complicity. 'Io voglio un pink gin,' she said.

'E il signor colonello?' the waiter asked.

Chastened by Audrey's rebuke, the signor colonello plumped for a pink gin too, although he would really have preferred a sherry. As the waiter wandered away, he wondered how he was going to get back into her good graces and decided that it had better be by way of politics, since she had started on this line herself.

'Do you really think that Tito will have a shot at Carinthia?' he asked.

'I beg your pardon; I'm afraid I didn't get that one,' Audrey said.

'I asked you if you really thought that Tito would have a shot at Carinthia,' Colonel Omicron said.

'Sorry,' Audrey said. 'Did I never tell you that I'm frightfully left-eared?'

'DO YOU REALLY THINK THAT TITO WILL HAVE A SHOT AT CARINTHIA?' Colonel Omicron shouted slowly, emphasizing each syllable.

'How should I know?' Audrey said.

'But, my dear, you said that you'd said that to the Field Marshal,' Colonel Omicron said.

'My poor Blinker, I've said so many things to the Field Marshal,' Audrey said.

'Careless talk, sir, I'm afraid.' One of the pipsqueak majors seated opposite was standing in front of Colonel Omicron waving a reproving wineglass. 'I'm afraid I couldn't help hearing what you were saying, sir, and I thought I'd better warn you that Tito is top secret. Walls have ears, sir, and all that sort of thing. Sorry, sir. G.S.I.(b)., you know.' The major smiled and walked picturesquely back to his place.

'Really, Blinker, you *are* naughty, aren't you?' Audrey said. 'You're compromising me, you know.'

'But look here, Audrey, you were talking about the same subject yourself a minute ago,' Colonel Omicron protested. 'You said that Alex himself had distinctly told you . . .'

'I didn't say Alex; I said the Field Marshal, because, although I don't know Alex, I know several Field Marshals, but I didn't say which Field Marshal, for reasons of security, Blinker,' Audrey said, wrinkling her nose as she sipped wryly at her cocktail. 'I only met Alex once, and it was at Ascot, I remember, and then I didn't really meet him because I thought he was Duff Cooper and I said, "Hello, Duff," and he said, "No, I am NOT Lord Dufferin," but of course he was frightfully friendly about it all.'

'I've no doubt he would be,' Colonel Omicron said.

'Of course, if you're going to get jealous,' Audrey said.

'I'm not getting jealous; I was merely making a

remark,' Colonel Omicron said, glaring at three lieutenant-colonels who had lined up opposite.

'Now you're being mean to me,' Audrey said,
drooping her lower lip and widening her eyes pa-
thetically. 'I don't know what you asked me out to
dinner for if it was only to be rude to me.'

'My dearest Audrey, I assure you . . .' Colonel
Omicron said.

'You can assure me as much as you like, but first
you're rude to me and then you're jealous.'

'Jealousy is the greatest compliment which a man
can pay to a woman,' Colonel Omicron said. 'But of
course I wasn't jealous,' he added.

'There you go again, Blinker,' Audrey said. 'You
make the most wonderfully inspiring remark to me
and then you go and spoil it all. Come clean,
Blinker: you *were* jealous, weren't you?'

'All right, then, I was,' Colonel Omicron said.

'Darling Blinker. I'm so glad,' Audrey said.
'After all, a girl prefers to be *liked* by the men who
take her out to dinner, especially when . . .'

'Especially when what?' Colonel Omicron asked.

'Especially when she'd rather go out with the man
in question than with any other man in Vienna,'
Audrey said, closing her eyes and making her eyelashes stand out in crescents of stiff little spikes.

'Oh, Audrey,' Colonel Omicron said.

'Now come along and don't get licentious,' Audrey
said, coming briskly out of her half swoon. 'Be an

angel, Blinker, and cycle along to the hall porter and ask him if he's found the compact I left here last Tuesday or it may have been a cigarette lighter.'

Reeling with love, Colonel Omicron walked along to the hall porter.

'Good evening, sir,' the hall porter said.

'Guten Abend,' Colonel Omicron said. 'Fräulein compact oder lighter here Dienstag oublié — I mean vergessen hat.'

'The young lady must have made a mistake, sir,' the hall porter said. 'Neither a compact nor a cigarette lighter has been found here since Tuesday, but young ladies often make mistakes, sir, especially when they are in love.'

'I'll tell you a secret,' Colonel Omicron said, unable to restrain his desire to confide in someone. 'These young chaps don't know anything about it, they haven't a clue; what girls like is chaps with a bit of experience, chaps who've knocked about the world a bit, men of the world, in fact.'

'I couldn't agree with you more, sir,' the hall porter said.

When Colonel Omicron got back to the bar, however, he found the three lieutenant-colonels sitting at the same table as Audrey, drinking double whiskies and sodas.

'Oh, Blinker, this is Pinky and this is Andrew and this is Ruffles,' Audrey introduced. 'I asked them over for a quick one, as you were such a long time.

After all, we're all in the Army, and I'm sure we've lots of interests in common.'

Colonel Omicron was certain that he had no interests in common with Pinky and Andrew and Ruffles, who all looked as though they were still wet behind the ears. He succeeded, however, in scraping up some sort of a grimace and sat down and gulped so energetically at his martini that some of it went up the back of his nose and made him choke.

'Hit him on the back somebody,' the lieutenant-colonel called Pinky said.

'Chap told me in India that the best thing to do in a case like that was to take off your shoes,' the lieutenant-colonel called Andrew said.

'Or drink the rest of your drink out of the wrong side of the glass just like hiccups,' the lieutenant-colonel called Ruffles said.

'Poor Blinker,' Audrey said. 'Somebody blow his nose for him like a dear.'

'I'm afraid I didn't manage to get either your compact or your lighter, Audrey,' Colonel Omicron said, with tears of gin still streaming down his cheeks. 'Chap said he hadn't got them. I asked him in a big way too.'

'That's all right, Blinker,' Audrey said. 'I remember now that I forgot them in the Bristol.'

The three lieutenant-colonels had, at Audrey's invitation, another three double whiskies-and-sodas, but Audrey told them not to bother about paying, as she said that Blinker had plenty of money, since he was a full colonel in Welfare. Pinky said that it was frightfully decent of him, sir, and Andrew said that he thought it frightfully decent of him, too, sir, but Ruffles merely asked if it was true that chaps in Welfare got paid for doing nothing, of which Colonel Omicron took rather a poor view, especially as Ruffles didn't call him 'sir.' However, after Colonel Omicron had paid out the money, they went away, although they all tried to make appointments with Audrey first, but Audrey said they'd better ring her up at the office, as she remembered dates better that way.

The waiters at the Kinsky all knew Audrey because she dined there every night of the week with a different escort. They were conducted, therefore, both with expedition and ceremony to the table which Colonel Omicron had reserved.

'Now, Blinker, I'm all yours,' Audrey said.

'Enfang sools,' Colonel Omicron said.

'Now, Blinker, tell me something interesting.' Audrey leaned across the table and looked enticingly at her host.

Colonel Omicron had always been a romantic. Twenty years ago, as a young officer, he had changed his underlinen three times a week in case he should be injured in a motor accident and rescued by a pretty girl who would have to undress him and put him to bed. Neither the motoring accident nor the pretty girl had ever happened, but only Mrs. Omicron, in Simla. Overseas service in wartime, with Mrs. Omicron doing a bit of queueing in Harrogate, had again raised hopes which had not been completely fulfilled until tonight. He determined, however, that he wasn't going to spoil things by rushing his fences.

'Do you like Vienna better or Rome?' he asked.

'I like Rome better than Vienna because in Rome you can get your hair done up till seven-thirty,' Audrey said.

'Salt?' he asked. 'Do you take salt with your soup?'

'Lashings,' Audrey said.

'They say that the English take more salt with their food than the Austrians,' Colonel Omicron said.

There was a silence during which they listened to a girl with a big nose at the next table saying to her companion: 'I could eat millions of eggs, simply millions.'

'Read Bernard Shaw's latest book?' Colonel Omicron asked.

'What was it called?' Audrey asked.

'I'm afraid I've forgotten the title,' Colonel Omicron said.

'I expect it was terrifically Shavian,' Audrey said.

'I expect so,' Colonel Omicron said.

'And I ate thirteen carrots,' the girl at the next table said.

'I say, Audrey, fun's fun and all that, but I don't want you to run away with the idea that I talk like this to every girl I take out,' Colonel Omicron said.

'Of course I don't, Blinker,' Audrey said.

'And I suppose you're the big, bad wolf,' the girl at the next table said.

'Heavens, there's Twingo,' Audrey said, her face lighting. 'Dining alone too. Mind if I drift over and speak to him?'

'Twingo darling, it's only you I love, at least for the moment it is,' Audrey said as she twirled in the rummage of the dance, tracing the simian twiddlings without effort, just as though she'd been at home, in the hush of Berkeley Square. 'Oh, I know you think I'm a shrew, but I'm a shrew with a nice nature, at least I think I am.'

Twingo did not answer, but danced on, wearing the solemn expression of coagulated gloom affected by those who make merry with their feet. Round and round the floor they swept, winding a way in and out of the other dancers, who also looked just as though they were about to vomit or to be executed. The orchestra wheezed out a treacle of Babylonian träumerei, the signature tune of the civilisation to save which young men had died with gaping bellies. Audrey closed her eyes and tilted her face.

'You're not cross with me because I'm out with that silly ass Blinker, are you?' she asked. 'Because honestly he means nothing to me. None of them mean anything to me and I only go out with them because you won't take me out.'

Her breath came on a waft of wine and lipstick, but it made no difference to Twingo, who once again did not answer, but merely patted her arm a little and then went on pushing her through fluid corridors of revolving brigadiers. Twingo did not know why he didn't love Audrey when there was every reason why he should love her. Audrey was so beautiful and young and rich, and Audrey loved him. But that was the way things had always worked out as far as he was concerned. He had never been able to fall in love with the girls who had fallen in love with him and the girls with whom he had been in love had never loved him. There had been the marchesa, of course, but the marchesa had merely been an excursion into excitement, like climbing Ben Nevis for the first time. He tried to think of the marchesa so that he shouldn't think of Maria, but her image eluded him and it was still of Maria he thought.

'Twingo darling, you're not listening to a single word I'm saying,' Audrey said, holding her cool face close to his, so that her hair brushed his cheek. 'You're still thinking about Maria, aren't you?'

The mention of her name by another made her

sound more accessible and the syllables soothed his mind like lint placed on a wound. He closed his eyes and tried to imagine that it was with Maria that he was dancing, with her hand in his and the touch of her dress against him; when he opened them again, he was still dancing with Audrey and they had bumped into a full colonel with teeth like a tank tread.

'I beg your pardon, sir,' he apologized to the colonel, and he apologized to Audrey as well for thinking about Maria when he ought to have been thinking about her. 'I'm ever so sorry, Audrey, but that's how things are.'

'You just can't help it, can you?' She was crying quietly, but she tried not to show it, smiling at him through the sparkle of her tears. 'Just as I can't help thinking about you. Ought to make one laugh like a drain if it didn't make one want to weep like one instead.' But for all her bravery her chin shook and the tears came tumbling down towards her mouth in silver pebbles. 'Oh, Twingo, life's a nonsense, isn't it, and as to what it all means, sometimes I haven't a clue, have you?' She caught at her grief with her tongue, sucking it ridiculously into her naughty red mouth. 'Do you know, at first I was glad when Hooky handed Maria back to the Russians that morning after breakfast because I thought it'd mean that I'd get you for myself and I knew that you loved her sitting there in the sunlight; but now

I'm sorry that he handed her back because I don't want you to be miserable, and that must mean that I love you if I don't want you to be miserable.'

'Audrey darling, you mustn't cry,' Twingo said, steering her discreetly past the full colonel, whose beaky-nosed consort was trying to hear what they were saying. 'I'm an awful swine really, and one day when I'm hanged for rape at the age of ninety you'll be awfully proud you didn't marry me.'

'And I'll become a tart, Twingo,' she said. 'Would you come and see me sometimes if I became a tart? Perhaps when I was a very old retired tart you would. Oh, Twingo, why is everything such a muddle at times?'

They danced on until her tears dried and she was able to powder her face without attracting people's notice.

'Now, Blinker, be an angel and explain to me all about the gold standard.' Riding back home with Colonel Omicron in the buzz-wagon, Audrey seemed to have recovered her spirits.

'The gold standard is based on gold,' Colonel Omicron began dismally. 'And of course silver comes into it as well, although I've never understood quite how, because it's all frightfully complicated.'

'On second thoughts I think you'd better tell me about trade winds,' Audrey said. 'I've always been a little vague about monsoons.'

'It all starts with hot air rising and cold air rushing in to take its place,' Colonel Omicron said.

'But why are they called "trade" winds, Blinker?' Collected in her corner, Audrey was obstinately academic.

'Because originally they helped trade, I suppose,' Colonel Omicron said. 'You know, blew the jolly old sailing ships along.'

'You've got it wrong, Blinker; that's the Gulf Stream,' Audrey said.

'I don't want to be rude, but how can the Gulf Stream *blow* ships along?' Colonel Omicron said.

'Well, *suck* them along, if you like it better,' Audrey said.

'I still don't think that the Gulf Stream comes into it at all,' Colonel Omicron said.

'Have it your own way, Blinker,' Audrey said. 'That's what the Russians are jealous of us for: because we own the Gulf Stream.'

'You mean, America owns the Gulf Stream,' Colonel Omicron said.

'Don't be silly, Blinker; you're thinking of the Panama Canal,' Audrey said.

'Perhaps I am,' Colonel Omicron said.

They rode the rest of the way in silence.

X

Wiener Frauen, Wiener Männer,
Wählen Körner, Seitz und Renner,

the electioneering placards pasted up by the Oester-
reichische Sozialistische Partei said, but Colonel
Nicobar paid no attention, because in the Herren-
gasse a pretty fair-haired girl had just passed him
with a proud high look on her face and it had made
him feel that he was getting old. Instead, to relieve
his feelings, he stuck his head out of the window of
his car and roared 'Verfluchter Schweinhund' at an
intrepid Austrian lorry-driver, although he was in-
stantly aware that Reverend Mother Auxilia would
not have approved, because she had told him, on
more than one occasion, that the future peace of the
world depended upon the unseen victories which
each individual was able to gain over his predisposi-
tion to greed, cowardice, and impatience. This
particular November morning, however, Colonel
Nicobar was not feeling capable of concern about
world affairs, because Senior Subaltern Quail had
just telephoned him at the Bundesministerium für
Inneres, which he had been visiting on official business, to say that Brigadier Catlock wanted to see him

immediately. The interruption had displeased him doubly: first, it meant that he would have to return later to the Bundesministerium in order to complete his enquiries, and secondly, he never liked being sent for by the brigadier, because it generally meant getting more work to do.

'The subject is Maria Bühlen,' the brigadier said as soon as Colonel Nicobar entered his office. 'Young Gideon tells me that you handed her over to the Russians more than a month ago.'

'Captain Gideon's information is correct, sir,' Colonel Nicobar said.

'I'm afraid between us Gideon and I have made a bit of a nonsense of this,' Brigadier Catlock said. 'Oh, it's my can all right, Hooky, and I'll carry it.' He smiled a brief smile which accentuated the weary lines on his face and made the colonel think that perhaps the brigadier wasn't such a bad chap after all and was probably just as overworked as he was. 'I know the Soviets asked for her all right, but it now appears that it's not official policy to repatriate political dissidents. And in any case she's a Volksdeutscher. Look here, Hooky, what exactly is a Volksdeutscher?'

'A Reichsdeutscher is a citizen of pre-thirteenth March, 1938, Germany,' Colonel Nicobar rattled off readily enough. 'A Volksdeutscher is a person of Germanic origin resident in a country other than Germany or Austria and accorded a privileged

114

status by Hitler when he overran those countries in which they were resident.'

'Sounds just all right to me, Hooky,' the brigadier said.

'Though whether there can technically be such a person as a Russian Volksdeutscher beats me because the Volga Germans were sent to Siberia long before there was any possibility of their being overrun.'

But Brigadier Catlock wasn't really listening.

'Chaliapin,' he said. 'I suppose he's dead now, or isn't he?' He got up and began to prance about the room, bawling out a noise which he imagined sounded like the *Volga Boat Song*. 'Come to think of it, these singer chaps must have an easy time of it. Wine, women, and song, whereas all we poor sods ever get nowadays is beer, bitches, and broadcasting. Vice seems to have gone down the drain like everything else.' He came and stood by Colonel Nicobar and laid his hand on his shoulder for a moment and then went and sat down again at his desk. 'Ever regretted becoming a soldier, Hooky?' he asked.

'Not so as you'd notice it,' Colonel Nicobar said.

'I once thought of becoming a parson, but I don't suppose I'd have been much good at being good.' They both smiled as they thought of Bishop Catlock, in blown-out lawn sleeves, preaching away about the Pentateuch. 'That arm of yours must be a bit of a nuisance to you at times, Hooky,' the brigadier said.

'It's not as difficult as it looks, you know,' the colonel said.

'All the same you might have found things easier in business, although I don't always envy those chaps with their Anthony Edens and their rolled umbrellas,' the brigadier said. 'Which reminds me: going to Blinker's cocktail party?'

'Not frightfully,' the colonel said.

'I'm not either,' the brigadier said and brought to an end their intimacy, which was the closest they had ever achieved. 'Well, Maria Bühlen's over and done with apparently and the least said soonest mended.'

Leaving the brigadier, the colonel decided that he wouldn't return to the Bundesministerium just yet, but would look in at his office first, in case something more important had turned up while he was out. He also decided that he would say nothing to Twingo about the mistake which had been made over Maria Bühlen, because it would only make the young man sadder. He didn't feel sad himself for very long, however, because a military band began to play again somewhere and he threw out his chest and marched again in 1914 to Mons, with young girls throwing flowers at him.

Nothing important had turned up at the office while he had been out except a routine order and the Rumanian general: the notice said that tropical kit would no longer be worn and the Rumanian general said that he was no longer looking for *sixty* thousand loyal Rumanians who had fought on the side of the Allies, but only for *six* thousand, as he had made a mistake in the nothings.

'Spiritually speaking, although I'm no spiritualist, sir, I think e's talking out of the back of is ead,' Sergeant Moonlight said.

However, the colonel left the Rumanian general to talk out of the back of his head to Senior Subaltern Quail, who seemed to like listening, and himself drove back to the Bundesministerium to resume his interrupted deliberations.

XI

With the light from the lamp casting a lovely glow on her face, Schwester Kasimira sat promoting the colonel's second-best battledress, because Colonel Nicobar had been only a lieutenant-colonel six months ago as he might be only a lieutenant-colonel again six months hence, because that was the way of the Army, popping up and popping down. Schwester Kasimira did not talk as she sewed, but kept her head bent over her work, because she was working to the greater glory of God. Watching her, Colonel Nicobar wondered if nuns really knew how wicked men of the world sometimes were and if they would speak of them if they did. Reverend Mother Auxilia seemed to have some rough ideas on the subject, of course, as he had gathered from watching her watch Twingo and himself counting the spirit ration when it came in from N.A.A.F.I. although there was nothing really very wicked in that. 'Every little betrayal, every little rhyming of conviction and convenience, every little selfishness, every little preference of immediate comfort to ultimate good hastens the coming of the next war,' Reverend Mother Auxilia had once said to him, as she sat embroidering a pink chasuble for use on special Sundays in Advent and Lent.

Reverend Mother Auxilia was watching him now, he felt sure, as she sat on the other side of the lamp, reading her breviary, as she had not always time to say her office in choir with the other nuns because she was too busy looking after the administration of the convent. She often came in and sat with him in the evenings now, and the colonel rather liked it, because with Audrey and Twingo always being out he felt lonely. Sometimes he wondered whether it was quite the drill to sit there drinking whisky while she was reading holy Latin words in her book right in front of him, but he supposed that she would have told him if she had objected.

The light from the lamp fell with friendliness on the nuns' habits and the colonel's red tabs and gay splash of medal ribbons. When Reverend Mother had finished saying matins and lauds for the next day, she looked at the lamp through half-closed eyes until she began to be able to imagine that it was a miniature moon, shining a timid brilliance onto their tiny world. Soon, however, and naturally enough since she was a nun, she was thinking of sanctifying grace, which also shone as a moon upon a world, and of how sad it was that so few men should attempt to correspond with it. She thought of this for some time before she decided to ask the colonel a question which had long been in her mind, because, although

119

she was an impatient nun, she was also a good nun, and her goodness often made her ashamed of her worldly knowledge.

'Tell me, Herr Oberst, why aren't you a Christian?' she asked.

'I'm not an official Christian, if that's what you mean, Reverend Mother,' the colonel said at length.

'There is no other way of being a Christian,' Reverend Mother said. 'Either one accepts official Christianity or one doesn't; private Christianity inevitably degenerates into heresy and licence.'

'Official Christianity hasn't got a very good record, has it?' the colonel said, a little angrily. 'Thinking men the world over have no more use for official Christianity.' He stopped as he saw the hurt on her face. 'Forgive me, Reverend Mother; I didn't intend to be offensive. I always look at things this way: all men are swine, but the trouble is to separate the swine from the swine.' He tried to reassure the nun with a smile, knowing that he had not expressed himself very well. 'You know, we have a very good rule in the Army: If you want to avoid unpleasantness, never talk about politics or religion.'

'You will pardon me, Herr Oberst, if I tell you that I am thinking that it is a very stupid rule, as politics and religion are the only subjects worth talking about, since one concerns our temporal welfare and the other our eternal welfare,' Reverend Mother said. 'And as I am not in the least interested in whether you eat more fish in England than we eat in Austria or whether your jet-propelled aeroplanes will be able to travel faster than the American jet-propelled aeroplanes, it is a rule which I do not intend to observe. As regards what you were saying about all men being swine and separating the swine from the swine, what you really ought to have said was that the difficulty was to separate from the swine the swine who try not to be swine from the swine that don't.' She looked sadly at Schwester Kasimira as she spoke, but Schwester Kasimira was still quietly sewing away and did not raise her head. 'Quite apart from that, Herr Oberst, you have made two statements: the first was that official Christianity hadn't got a very good record and the second was that thinking men the world over haven't got any more use for official Christianity. Oh, it's all right, you don't need to mind Schwester Kasimira: her faith is as secure as my own.'

'Look here, Reverend Mother, I don't want to hurt your feelings,' Colonel Nicobar said.

'Herr Oberst, if you were one of my nuns, I should order you under holy obedience to hurt my feelings,' Reverend Mother said. 'As you are not a nun, however, I can only request you to hurt them. Please, Herr Oberst; I am not accustomed to being kept waiting.'

'The two questions are really one, Reverend

Mother,' the colonel said, looking at the lamp rather than at Reverend Mother as he spoke, so that he would not have to observe the effect of his words on her expression. 'I have only to remind you of the Middle Ages, to prove the truth of my first statement: the Borgias, the quarrels about the succession to the Papacy, the immoral lives of the clergy, the crimes committed by worldly prelates lusting for power, the tortures of the Spanish Inquisition, all that deceit, ambition, and cruelty does not reflect the spirit of Christ which even the man in the street knows was sweet and gentle. And Richelieu,' he concluded. 'There's a chap for you.'

Schwester Kasimira raised her head slowly from her sewing. The colonel thought that she looked very tired and plain and stupid.

'And how does the man in the street know that the spirit of Christ was sweet and gentle?' she asked.

'He's read it in the Bible, of course,' Colonel Nicobar said. 'Matthew, Mark, Luke, John.'

'I do not think that the man in the street is reading his Bible quite as much as you are perhaps liking to believe,' Schwester Kasimira said. 'And even if they do read the Bible, who kept it safe for them down the centuries, when men were being so wicked? Was it not the Church, whose official representatives were so often giving such very bad examples of the teachings of their Master? But there were other official representatives whose names did not get into

122

the history books, humble priests and nuns who did God's will, although some even of them became famous, like Santa Teresa of Avila and San Juan de la Cruz and Santa Rosa of Lima. You see, Herr Oberst, I do not think that you are quite understanding. The Lord made the Church out of mortal men and women and He did not say that they would be without sin, but only that He would guide the Church, so that it would not err and that the light would still shine from it. That the light still shines from a Church that has often had such wicked leaders is surely a proof of its divine mission rather than the reverse. No, Herr Oberst, God will not let us fail,' she said, and bent her head again and went on with her sewing.

But the colonel thought that he had heard all that sort of thing before.

'Take this last war, then,' he said. 'For the second time in less than twenty-five years Christian has fought against Christian, Catholic against Catholic. And what have the cardinals and the archbishops and the bishops had to say about it? Has one single significant utterance come from their lips? Has any one of them uttered a clear statement that sinful men could understand and be guided by? Has any German archbishop told the Germans that it was a crime to launch flying bombs and rockets against the city of London? Has any Italian bishop spoken a fearless thing? Has any English archbishop or

123

bishop dared to condemn the area-bombing of Berlin and the burning alive of German babies with phosphorus bombs? Has the Holy Father ever spoken one clear unambiguous truth that could be understood of the people, by the harlot in her doorway as well as by the pontiff in his palace? Has any cardinal cried out the clean, true, cool gospel of Christ that even men in their taverns respect?

'Oh, I know, there have been pronouncements, condemnations of sin in general terms, but tired, bewildered, and unhappy men want more than that. They want to be guided, instructed, given an ideal. At present neither the victors nor the vanquished know what to believe in: science tells them one thing and religion tells them another, and in their bewilderment they abandon metaphysical conjecture and turn to the material; the victors bury their heads in their old philosophy of a good time and trains with restaurant cars, and the vanquished have no time to worry about a philosophy at all because all their energies are used up in the struggle to exist. No cardinal or archbishop comes along to dispel their doubts and uncertainties and to prove to them that religion is not the phoney nonsense they honestly believe it to be. For you must not make the mistake of imagining, Reverend Mother, that all worldlings are in bad faith and insincere. Many of them, I think, are as sincere in their unbelief as you and Schwester Kasimira are in your faith: they are only too willing to be converted to official Christianity, but first of all the representatives of official Christianity have got to prove to them that the Church of Christ stands for social justice, honesty, kindness to the weak, and that its interpretation of the word "sin" is not, as the common man honestly believes it is, solely in terms of alcohol and sex. That is what you require to prove to the world, Reverend Mother, before men will come willingly to the wedding feast, and to do so I rather think that you will require tongues more eloquent and minds more alert than those belonging to the country bumpkins Holy Mother Church continues to consecrate as bishops. Forgive me if I have hurt your feelings, but you asked me to speak plainly, and please believe that I am as anxious as you for the world to hear some glad new thing.'

'Thank you, Herr Oberst, for having spoken your thought so plainly,' Reverend Mother said, and then they both saw that the Russian colonel had entered the room, with Schwester Michaela by his side, and even Schwester Kasimira looked up from her work and smiled, because she thought that the Russian colonel looked tired and she was sorry for him.

'You are a little wrong,' the Russian colonel said slowly in difficult English. 'The victors are not all burying their heads. In Russia it will be a long time before we think about trains with restaurant cars. In Russia we used to say that Peter the Great was a bad man because he was cruel; now in Russia we are saying that Peter the Great was a good man because he wanted Russia to be great.' He smiled as he said these words, but it was impossible to tell from his smile whether he himself approved or disapproved of their sentiment. 'But that is not what I am coming to talk about. I am coming to talk about a much different matter. I am coming to talk about Maria Bühlen. I am coming to tell you that she has escaped. Evidently she was not believing all the promises which we were making her.'

'And let me tell you that I should not have been believing them either, Herr Oberst,' Reverend Mother Auxilia said. 'And let me tell you also that I am very glad that she has escaped.'

'Perhaps we are being a little unkind to Herr Oberst Piniev,' Schwester Kasimira said. 'Perhaps the Herr Russische Oberst himself believed the promises which he made on behalf of his Government. In any case, I do not see that it will do any of us benefit to go on distrusting one another.'

'I beg your pardon, Herr Oberst Piniev,' Reverend Mother Auxilia said immediately. 'I had no right to speak as rudely as I did and I shall ask our Lord to forgive me.'

'It is of no matter at all,' Colonel Piniev said. 'I merely am coming to tell you that Maria Bühlen has escaped and to ask you if she has again taken shelter in your convent. Oh, I know what you are thinking,

Reverend Mother. You are wondering how I know that she ever took shelter in your convent, since I was not appearing to know that night. Well, I did not know that night, but I knew the next morning, and it was not Herr Oberst Nicobar who told me, so that you need not be looking crossly at him. We Russians have little ways of finding things out, such as counting the number of nuns who were praying in your convent *before* Maria Bühlen was handed over to us and again counting the number of nuns who were praying in your convent *after* Maria Bühlen was handed over to us, so you will see that there is nothing very complicating about it. But we shall let gonebyes be gonebyes, Reverend Mother, and look only to the future, which unfortunately does not seem as though it were going to be so very much more beautiful than the past. Reverend Mother, please answer me this question and this time I shall believe you.'

'I did not lie last time, Herr Oberst,' Reverend Mother Auxilia said.

'Oh, no, you did not lie; you merely allowed me to be searching your convent for a lie,' Colonel Piniev said. 'That is what, I think, you call a white lie. Oh, there is no need to look ashamed. Christians are not the only people who fail to live up to their creed: communists fail, too, sometimes.' He smiled quite gaily at them all, although the lines round his grey eyes made him look tired. 'Then I am believing that this time Maria Bühlen is not hid-

127

den away in your convent and dressed up as a nun as lovely as Schwester Michaela here?'

They all laughed together, forgetting momentarily as they had once forgotten them before, their antagonisms in their common sense of the ridiculous. Watching the beauty which briefly lit their unhappy faces, Colonel Nicobar wondered if it lit also his own, and then saw that Schwester Michaela, who always looked beautiful, was blushing, perhaps because it was not so very long since she had been at dances, with young men whispering in her ear.

'No, this time she is not here, Herr Oberst Piniev, neither dressed as a nun nor as an ordinary young woman of the world,' Reverend Mother Auxilia said.

'Then this time I shall be believing you,' Colonel Piniev said.

'Thank you,' Reverend Mother Auxilia said. 'Won't you sit down and talk to us for a little?'

Colonel Piniev sat down. Tonight he was not wearing his ordinary high-buttoned tunic and blue breeches with a thin red stripe; instead, he was wearing a khaki smock and baggy breeches which were also khaki. There were medal ribbons on his breast, two of which were the same, red and grey, red and grey. Colonel Nicobar wanted to ask him what they were for and whether they had anything to do with Leningrad or Stalingrad, but didn't like to in front of the nuns, who weren't militarily minded. So they all sat in silence trying to think up something to say to one another until Colonel Nicobar asked the Russian colonel if he would like a glass of whisky.

'Scottish vodka, no tap heels,' Colonel Piniev said, swallowing the contents of his glass at a gulp. 'Good health, mud in your eye, same again.'

Reverend Mother Auxilia turned her kind lined old face towards Colonel Piniev and looked at him earnestly. 'Herr Oberst, I am beginning to believe that you are a man of broad understanding and human sympathy and accordingly I am encouraged to ask you a question which I should not otherwise have thought of asking you,' she said.

'Reverend Mother Auxilia may be asking me any questions which she may be wanting to, although I hope she will not be asking any indiscreet questions,' Colonel Piniev said.

'You must not embarrass the colonel,' Colonel Nicobar said. 'You must remember that he is under very strict orders.'

Everyone looked so uncomfortable when he had said this that Colonel Nicobar wondered whether he ought to have made the remark. He had been frightened, however, lest Reverend Mother should ask the Russian colonel a question to which he ought not to reply and which he might answer out of a mistaken sense of politeness and so incur the displeasure of his superiors. They all sat with sketchy smiles on

their faces, but behind their smiles they were thinking
of the Russian Secret Police and of the terrible things
it was reputed to do to Russians who said anything
against Soviet doctrines and of Colonel Piniev sitting
there looking so nice and friendly and human and
with eyes and hair and nose just like themselves and
still being spied upon by the Russian Secret Police.

'Even in the hot of battle I am sure that Colonel
Nicobar is not forgetting the orders of his general
and I am too a soldier and so I shall not be forgetting
the orders of my general even in the hot of peace,'
Colonel Piniev said.

'Thank you, Herr Oberst Piniev,' Reverend
Mother Auxilia said. 'Herr Oberst, when you came
in just now, we were in the middle of a very serious
discussion. I had been asking Herr Oberst Nicobar
why he was not a Christian and now I am going to
ask you the same question. Herr Oberst Piniev, why
is it that you are not a Christian?'

Colonel Nicobar watched Colonel Piniev's expression closely, but there was not the slightest expression
of a sneer as he sat there thinking over what form
his reply should take.

'I suppose I am not being a Christian because I am
being a communist,' he said. 'But do not let that
offend you, Reverend Mother, because sometimes,
in spite of what our leaders say, I am thinking that
both true communists and true Christians are trying
to achieve the same purpose.'

'The Holy Father is not thinking so, but please go on all the same,' Reverend Mother said.

'If you will be listening a little I shall be trying to tell you,' Colonel Piniev said. 'I was very young when the revolution broke out in Russia, let us be saying about twenty years old. I was wanting the revolution, not because I was tired of the war against Germany, but because I thought that it was the only way of making the Russian people happy. I knew that the Czar would never make the people happy, neither the nobles, neither their beautiful womans in silks, neither even the priests, although they said that they believed the religion of Jesus Christ Who was wanting to make all mens happy. So I became a revolutionary, which was not very difficult, because my father had been a revolutionary before me, only my father was a pom-pom revolutionary, because he tried to blow up the Czar's railway train; but I was a kind revolutionary and did not want to kill anyone, not even the rich peoples who had been unkind to the poor peoples, but only to make all peoples happy together in Russia, whether it was sun in summer or snow in winter. I was never wanting to murder the rich peoples and to steal their jewels and to throw priests naked into frozen rivers and to watch them drown under the ice. I was wanting to be a kind revolutionary, I am saying, but Russia stamped out my revolution just as the Church has stamped out the spirit of Christ out of Christianity. Please do not

131

be offended, Reverend Mother: I know that you are trying to be a true Christian just as I am trying to be a true communist, only events and other men's selfishness are too strong for us, as they were too strong for Saint Francis.'

'I am glad that you have heard of Saint Francis, Herr Oberst,' Schwester Kasimira said. 'I think that he was a very beautiful saint.'

'I chose Saint Francis for my patron because I was confirmed on the fourth of October,' Schwester Michaela said, with a deliberate downward glance of her eyes which made Colonel Nicobar wonder whether she still found it difficult not to look in mirrors.

'Let's leave Saint Francis out of it,' Reverend Mother Auxilia said. 'Personally I have always thought him just a little bit sentimental; instead of all his preaching to the birds he might have gone and preached to the Pope, like our Holy Mother Saint Walburga of Graz. But what I do want to say to Herr Oberst Piniev is that it is quite incorrect to say that the Church has stamped the spirit of Christ out of Christianity. Whatever the personal failings of individual popes, the teaching of the Church has always been the teaching of Christ: thou shalt love the Lord thy God with all thy heart, and with all thy mind, and with all thy soul, and thy neighbour as thyself. That is the difference between your failure and ours, Herr Oberst: we still go on teaching and trying and praying, whereas if communism ever had a doctrine of equality, it has long ago abandoned it and preaches now only greater power for Russia.'

'Your teaching is not seeming, then, to have had a much lot of effect,' Colonel Piniev said, a little less patiently than before. 'The communist doctrine does not state that it is wrong to kill the enemies of communism whom it is considering as the enemies of progress, but the Christian doctrine does state that it is wrong not to love your enemies, and still German and Italian Catholics go bombing British and American Catholics and British and American Catholics come bombing German and Italian Catholics back, and none of them think that it is extraordinary because they have for so long been disobeying their Lord in this matter that they find it quite natural. The leaders on both sides say that it is about the things of the spirit that they are fighting, but the peoples themselves know that it is about oil and exports and imports, and still the peoples do not think that it is extraordinary because they are knowing that nobody is really caring very much about what the Lord is saying. Whereas in Russia, when we are fighting about oil, we say that we are fighting about oil.'

'That is not quite correct, colonel,' Colonel Nicobar said, deciding to abandon diplomacy and say bang out what he thought. 'Not only has Soviet Russia never told the truth to the world, she has also never told it to her own people. Why has the Russian people never been given the rightful account of the British and American war effort? Why have they not been told of the source of supply of so many of the guns, aeroplanes, and munitions with which they conquered the Germans? Why have they not been told of the very real and genuine admiration of the British and American peoples for the Red Army? And why are the equalitarian doctrines of communism no longer taught in Russia, where a Russian comrade general can get better rations than other people and where skilled technicians and government officials can give their children a better education than the common pleb?

'Shall I tell you what intelligent British and Americans are beginning to think? We are beginning to think that Russia is concerned only with the future of Russia as she was concerned only with the future of Russia when she made her hangman's plot with Hitler in 1939. We are beginning to think worse than that: we are beginning to think that the leaders of Russia are deliberately keeping the people of Russia in ignorance of the ideals and aims animating the Western Powers; we are beginning to think that the leaders of Russia are using the communist party in other countries to exploit discontent abroad and to act as a fifth column in the event of a third world war. For the threat of war comes now only from one power, colonel, and that power is Soviet

Russia. And that fact, colonel, sitting there with your whisky-and-soda in your hand, you must know fully as well as I do.'

'Shall I be saying that I am not very high in the councils of my nation and so am not knowing the thoughts which are lying in the minds of those who are directing the destinies of Soviet Russia?' Colonel Piniev said. 'Shall I be saying, too, that distrust can be coming from two sides as well as from one? Shall I be saying also that the attitude which the Western Powers adopted towards my country in the period coming immediately after our revolution did not make the Russians think the Western Powers were their friends? Shall I be saying that we in Russia knew that you were not hating us because we were the enemies of your Christ, but because you were thinking that we were the enemies of the accumulation of wealth and fat business men driving about in big motor cars with beautiful womans? Shall I be saying that in human quarrels both sides are always a little right and that both sides are always greatly in the wrong? We have both made mistakes, perhaps, but with a little understanding and self-sacrifice on both our parts, perhaps we might learn to work for the peace of the world which I should like you to believe that my country is desiring as earnestly as yours.'

'Thank you, colonel,' Colonel Nicobar said. 'You put your view with clarity. The trouble is that

135

revolutions always tend to attempt to export themselves: Napoleon, Hitler, and Mussolini, they all made the same mistake.'

'Pax Christi in regno Christi,' Reverend Mother Auxilia said. 'That is the only thing which can save the world. Herr Oberst Piniev, I do not quite know if you have really answered my question.'

'I have been telling you that I am not being a Christian because I am being a communist,' Colonel Piniev said. 'I shall also be telling you one thing more: if Christians had always obeyed the teachings of their Master, there would have been no need of communism. If the rich had always been kind to the poor, if the strong had always been gentle with the weak, if money and land and beautiful maidens had been able to be left lying about with only God's grace to guard them, if the stained glass in cathedrals had really reflected the aspirations of men and women living outside them, if every priest who stood at an altar had really been having the image of Christ engraved on his heart, then there would have been no need for Stalin and Molotov and all these men who are now making you so frightened.'

'Peace on earth to men of good will,' Schwester Kasimira said. 'That is indeed what our Lord promised.'

'But don't you see that if men and women were like that there'd be no need for God's Church at all?' Reverend Mother Auxilia said. 'And communists

136

can't possibly do *without* God what Christians have failed to do *with* God.'

'It's all very difficult, I admit,' the Russian colonel said.

Nobody said very much after that, although they sat on for a little exchanging banalities, Colonel Nicobar, who owed loyalty to the sprawl of a tired Empire, the Russian colonel, who owed loyalty to the new terror, and the three nuns, who owed loyalty to Christ, Who had so often been betrayed. Watching the quick way they comprehended one another when they spoke of trivial things, Colonel Nicobar wondered if it was indeed possible for them to share philosophy as they shared the wind, the rain, and the stars, which was the common finger of God upon them. Outside the hoot of an engine sounded far away behind the Wiener Wald and made the colonel think of his childhood, when he had listened from a tucked-in bed to the rattle of railway trucks in a darkness which Jesus made safe.

On his way up to bed the colonel looked into the chapel and found Reverend Mother Auxilia praying in front of the tabernacle, which was hung with red curtains, because the next day was the feast of a martyr. The colonel knew that she was praying for the peace of the world and the conversion of Russia, so he knelt down at the back of the chapel and tried to pray for the peace of the world and the conversion of Russia too, but it was so long since he had prayed that the words wouldn't come, so he tried to do a little holy thinking instead. Even this he found difficult and when he caught himself reflecting what a very much better brigadier he would have made than Brigadier Catlock, he concluded that his contemplation was unlikely to advance the spiritual welfare of himself or of others. So he rose and tiptoed out again, leaving Reverend Mother Auxilia with her straight back still praying and the sanctuary lamp sending down a round of shine on her veil.

XII

THE FEAST OF THE IMMACULATE CONCEPTION, which the nuns called die Unbefleckte Empfängnis, came and went, and Christmas came, too, with midnight Mass in the chapel, and the priest in white vestments, and the deacon chanting the gospel in a haze of happy incense, and the nuns all standing up in their stalls with their hands folded beneath their cloaks, listening to the Latin joy. The colonel did not really understand very much of the Mass, but he understood the meaning of the priest's blessing at the end all right. Not only to the nuns did that blessing go, but to the city and to the world as well, to the homeless on the cold highways, to babes in their cots and to old men on their deathbeds, to Audrey and Twingo doing a rhumba in the Kinsky, and to Stalin in the Kremlin. Then the enchantment vanished from the sanctuary and the priest came in again in his glossy black cassock and knelt down to make his thanksgiving with his collar sticking up too high at the back. The colonel felt that he could have gone on kneeling in all that peace for ever, but Schwester Kasimira came gliding up to him and said that a man wanted to speak to him on

139

the telephone and that he sounded so angry she was sure he must be a general.

It was, of course, Brigadier Catlock ringing up from his own mess.

'Look here, Hooky, fun's fun, but what's all this I hear about a trainload of Jugoslav Volksdeutsche arriving at Aspang Station?' the brigadier asked, his voice vibrating with rage.

'Volksdeutsche?' Colonel Nicobar repeated. 'I'm afraid I don't understand, sir.'

'Of course, you don't understand. I don't understand. Nobody understands. We're not paid to understand. We're only simple soldiers, Hooky, not diplomatists who can run round to George Bernard Shaw and ask him to read their bloody teacups.' The brigadier continued fluently for several seconds in basic Catlock. 'Simple soldiers, that's what we are, Hooky, the chaps who've got to bite on the bullet and sleep in the mud and pretend we love it. But that's not all we've got to do these days, Hooky. Every time a little Socialist runt with a running snout gets up in the House of Commons to ask some damfool question about Austria, we've got to be ready to brief the yellow-bellied baboon of a cabinet minister that's got to answer him. In other words, ploo sa shonge ploo say lamaime shows. And sooner or later some shocking little fellow's going to get up and ask a question about why these Jug Volksdeutsche are allowed to come into Austria.'

'But they're not allowed to come into Austria, sir,' Colonel Nicobar said. 'The Displaced Persons Division has made that perfectly clear. The Jugs have no business to expel them and the Russians have no business to allow them in through their Zone.'

'All that doesn't matter a hoot in hell,' the brigadier said. 'What does matter is that they mayn't be Volksdeutsche . . .'

'But, sir, you've just said that they were Volksdeutsche,' the colonel said.

'What does it matter what I say?' the brigadier roared on. 'What does it matter what anybody says? And how do I know that they are Volksdeutsche? How does anybody know they're Volksdeutsche? And what, when all's said and done is a Volksdeutscher, anyway?'

'A Volksdeutscher, sir, is a person of Germanic origin . . .' Colonel Nicobar began.

'Look here, Hooky, how do you expect me to say what I want to say when you keep on so rudely interrupting me?' the brigadier blistered, none the less effectively for being invisible. 'Who cares what a Volksdeutscher is, anyway? The point, my dear Watson, is that they may not be Volksdeutsche. They may be Croats, Slovenes, Chetniks, and Ustashis pretending to be Volksdeutsche. Got you there, haven't I, Hooky? Always remember that a chap's got to look below the surface. Look below the surface, that's my motto, and you'll never go far

141

wrong. The point is this, Hooky: these chaps may be rotters coming across with their pockets stuffed with anti-fascist propaganda. They may be dirty whites, Hooky.'

'And what if they turn out to be Volksdeutsche pretending to be Croats, Slovenes, and Ustashis?' Colonel Nicobar asked.

'Don't be such a damned fool, Hooky,' the brigadier snapped. 'Why on earth should a Croat pretend to be a Volksdeutscher? No, don't tell me: I don't want to know. What I do want to know is whether they've got any potential fifth columnists among them, fascist cads who've come along to make trouble, in other words, to conduct subversive activities, which is your job, although you don't appear to know it.'

'And what if they're communist cads, sir, who've also come along to make trouble?' Colonel Nicobar asked.

'Look here, Hooky, I haven't got all night to stand here arguing the toss,' the brigadier said. 'Believe it or not, I've got one of those financial boys with me and we're having a very interesting argument about the Polish zloty. You're a lucky chap, Hooky, although you don't know it. You've only got to keep subversive activities in your head, whereas I've got to know everything from historic monuments and fine arts to navigation on the Danube. You can thank your lucky stars you're not a brigadier, Hooky, old boy. Now don't stand there arguing the toss, but be a good chap and run along and do what I've asked you to do.'

'Do what, sir?' the colonel asked.

'Do the bloody thing, of course,' the brigadier barked, and rang off.

At first the colonel was so angry that he sat down and smoked a cigarette, deliberately postponing the undefined action which Brigadier Catlock wished him to take. As his rage cooled, however, he concluded that the brigadier must intend him to visit Aspang Station and ascertain whether the displaced persons who had just arrived in Vienna were Jugoslav Volksdeutsche, Croats, or Slovenes. To do this, he would require a car, and he was wondering how on earth to get a car at one o'clock on Christmas morning when he looked up to find that Schwester Kasimira was standing beside him, watching him with anxious eyes.

'Was the Herr General very angry with you?' she asked.

'It wasn't a general; it was a brigadier,' he said. 'You know, Schwester, in the Army it's not the generals who are unpleasant: the generals and the privates are all right; it's the people in between who stink.' He saw at once that she did not understand his joke and wondered if it had been ill-bred of him to use the word 'stink' when addressing a nun. 'Chap who was at Anzio said much the same thing,' he

143

floundered on, in an endeavour to redeem his gaffe. 'Chap asked him whether the battle was pretty terrible and the first chap answered: "Oh, the battle was all right, but, my God, the people!"' He realised at once, however, that he had only made things worse by profanity, even if it had been between quotes. 'I'm afraid you'll have to excuse me this evening, Schwester,' he said. 'My silly tongue seems to be running away with me.'

'I am thinking that you are very tired, Herr Oberst, and that it is very unkind of your brigadier, if that's what you call him, to telephone to you and make you unhappy,' Schwester Kasimira said. 'But when you are unhappy, Herr Oberst, you can always make yourself happy again by offering your unhappiness up as a gift to the Lord.'

At first, her words seemed ridiculous to him, unctuous even, but as he pondered them he began to think that he understood what she meant. After all, it was perhaps more sensible to attempt to do something supernatural with one's troubles than to try to annihilate them by blasting and blinding like a coal-heaver. Watching the gadarene swarms surging along the pavements of cities, he had sometimes wondered what incentive each had to live, since so obviously neither honour nor delight could be his here below.

Football matches, sex, cinema, guzzling, and golf, these had seemed to be some of the opiates which they took to hide from themselves the dreadful knowledge that they could never either matter or be happy. Perhaps some of them chose Schwester Kasimira's way, glorying in their discomfort because they knew that Jesus Christ hadn't stayed at the Ritz either. Perhaps there *were* unknown saints, Saint Ignatius Loyolas queuing at bus stops and Saint Augustines of Hippo giving up their seats in the tram. The thought made him briefly happy, seeming to consecrate some of the aridity of his soldiering.

'You're all right, Schwester,' he said, patting her arm. 'Don't you pay any attention to a rascal like me.'

'But you are not a rascal, Herr Oberst,' she informed him gravely. 'Reverend Mother Auxilia and all the other nuns pray for you a lot. We hope that one day the Lord will let you see the light, and in the meantime we are thinking that you are a very nice man.'

Her little speech touched him. He wondered if anyone else in the whole wide world ever cared whether he saw the light. His wife certainly not, idling at Roehampton, nor his daughters either, learning to be tarts at a young ladies' exclusive academy. To hide his emotion he took up the telephone and dialled the number of the car company.

There was, as perhaps was to be expected, no officer on duty, but only a Private Lavender, who was consistently uninspired. The colonel tried to

follow Schwester Kasimira's advice and super-
naturalize his exasperation, but as the process
seemed to make neither himself more persuasive
nor Private Lavender more receptive, he was soon
back at language more easily understood by soldiery,
although he kept back the earthy words, because
Schwester Kasimira was still standing beside him.

'Say "sir" when you speak to an officer,' he
began to bellow. 'Now, Lavender, listen to me:
this is Colonel Nicobar speaking, and I've got to
have a car at once, and it's got to have four wheels
with four unpunctured tyres on them, and the igni-
tion's got to work properly, and it's got to take me
immediately to Aspang Station to grill some Jug
Volksdeutsche who have just arrived. Never mind
about how the word's spelt, but get me a car. Get
me a taxi, get me anything. Of course, I've got
priority: get it in your turnip brain that it's much
more important that I should have a car to go to
Aspang than a lot of frivolous young women drinking
mother's ruin at the Kinsky and the Bag o' Nails.
Yes, Lavender, it's an order.'

He banged down the receiver and said to Schwester Kasimira before she could reproach him with
his impatience: 'I'm sorry, Schwester, but one has
got to express oneself with a certain amount of
forceful clarity when giving orders to the British
private soldier.'

'Bitte schön, Herr Oberst, but I could not help

understanding what your brigadier was saying to
you on the telephone,' Schwester Kasimira said.
'Bitte schön, Herr Oberst, but it was about Jugoslav
Volksdeutsche, was it not?'

'We hope that it was about Jugoslav Volksdeutsche, Schwester,' the colonel said. 'They're
poor wretches who've been pitchforked over the
frontier by the Jugs, because they won't allow people
of Germanic origin to go on living in Jugoslavia. The
Russians ought never to have let them in, of
course.'

'But the Russians *have* let them in, Herr Oberst,
and they've got immortal souls and poor bodies that
feel hunger and cold,' Schwester Kasimira said.
'Please, Herr Oberst, to let Schwester Michaela and
myself come with you in the car to the station. We
can take a little food with us and perhaps there will
be other works of mercy which we shall be able to
perform. Bitte schön, Herr Oberst.'

'The attention of all ranks is drawn to the rule
that unauthorized Austrian civilians are not allowed
to ride in W.D. transport,' the colonel had read only
that morning, but he was sure that quite a few senior
officers were, at this very moment, rolling up the
Mariahilferstrasse with young, smooth, silken, and
co-operative Gräfinnen in the back of their staff cars,
and if they could do that, surely he could drive a
couple of nuns to bring comfort to the homeless and
disinherited. 'All right, I'll take you,' he said.

147

He did not know where they got the food they brought with them to the car, or the hot coffee either, but their sacrifice of their own meagre stores made him ashamed and he ran to the larder and extracted some tins of corned beef and sardines, which he added to their supplies. 'God will repay you a thousandfold one day,' Schwester Kasimira said, and the colonel nearly said that he didn't like that sort of ledger-account charity, and then reflected that he might like it one day very much, indeed, when he was on the mat for the last time, answering for all his compromissions, incontinences, sloths, indolences, and earthy words.

The two nuns sat in the back of the car with the muddle of their packages and tins on their laps and the colonel sat beside the driver. It was a cold night with snow on the ground which had melted in places and frozen again to ice. As they crossed the Karlsplatz, snowflakes began to fall in a moving muslin against the windows and the windscreen. Around them the fireless houses towered in desolation with their unlighted windows like shut eyes, and the wind moaned in the slates, and the starless sky stretched on to empty Hungary and Russia. On the Mariahilferstrasse a whore or two in their primitive parsley stood beneath lamp-posts touting for doughboys and a notice said WÄSCHEREI FÜR GESCHEITE FRAUEN, and the snow went on falling soundlessly.

The green light at the entrance to the station fell on the faces of British soldiers arguing in broken German with Russian soldiers. The British soldiers were saying that, as the Russians had allowed the train in through their zone, it was the Russians' responsibility to find accommodation in one of their camps for the Jugoslav Volksdeutsche, and anyway, it was a Russian responsibility to repatriate Jugoslavs from Vienna nicht wahr, and the Russians were saying Jugoslavs ja, aber Jugoslav Volksdeutsche nicht, and that Aspang was a British station nicht wahr. There were some French soldiers there, too, nicht wahr-ing away on their own account, because the train had in the first instance been run into the Westbahnhof, which was a French station, and the Russians were trying to make them responsible as well.

The colonel was not long in ascertaining what had really happened, especially as he had guessed half the truth already. For some time past the Jugoslavs had been expelling Volksdeutsche from Jugoslavia, sending them into the British Zone of Austria through the Rosenbach Tunnel. The British, whose camps for Displaced Persons were already full and threatened with further infiltrations of Jews from eastern Europe, had given orders that all persons other than Austrians returning from Jugoslavia, or genuine displaced persons in transit from Jugoslavia to another country, were to be turned back at the

149

frontier, and had indicated that it was the duty of the Jugoslavs to keep their own Volksdeutsche, pending official decision as to their disposal. The Jugoslavs had then tried the experiment of driving isolated groups of Volksdeutsche over the hills, ordering them to inform the British authorities that they were Austrians. This procedure, through the vigilance of the British military and intelligence authorities, had, in turn, been largely abandoned, and now the Jugoslavs had sent a trainload of Volksdeutsche direct to Vienna.

As usual, these Volksdeutsche had been driven during the night from their homes by Jugoslav soldiers who had given them no time to collect their belongings. They had been, most of them without food or drink, four or five days on the train, which had been driven into Vienna via Hungary and the Russian Zone of Austria. The Russians were now refusing to let them leave the train until one of the three other Allied Powers had agreed to house them, and both the British and the French had refused to do so, not because they lacked pity, but because they knew that, if they accepted fifteen hundred Volksdeutsche today, Tito would be tempted to send them fifteen thousand tomorrow. It was a nice case between the bowels of compassion and the common sense which was also compassion.

'Miserere mei, Deus, secundum magnam misericordiam tuam,' Schwester Kasimira murmured as she walked with the colonel and Schwester Michaela along the frozen platform towards the train. Two Russian soldiers with fixed bayonets and round furry caps and big heavy overcoats were on guard, but they did not attempt to prevent the nuns and the colonel passing up the platform. Facing each other they stood, with their big feet in the snow. Five years ago they had been schoolboys and now they were hairless, close-cropped young men blearing at suffering with no understanding in their eyes. History, history, history, the colonel's shoes sang as they crunched on the snow, and how unhistorical it looked when seen in the happening, and what a mismanaged word it was, befouled by journalists and politicians. A few of the passengers had got out of the train and were walking up and down the platform with their hands in their pockets. One of them was a young priest and another was a Jew in a belted overcoat with a turf of fur on the collar. Both Schwester Kasimira and Schwester Michaela bowed to the priest, but the priest didn't bow back because he couldn't see them through the thicket of the Jew's big collar.

The nuns weren't alone in their wish to help the distressed. Other nuns were there as well, and British officers and N.C.O.'s and an Austrian relief agency, distributing hot soup and platefuls of lentils to the hungry and the cold. During the journey three old men had died of frostbite and their corpses had been thrown onto the platform, where they lay, pathetic and shrunken, with their eyes staring and the wind flapping in their thin clothes, because there were no blankets to cover them. A woman who had gone off her head was screaming and children were wailing as they woke up in the night, wondering why they were cold and hungry.

The colonel left the nuns to set about their business and himself set about his, working his way up the train from the near end to the far. Most of the compartments stank like sewers, as many of the passengers had been too frozen to be able to leave the train, but the colonel went through them all, because he wanted to be able to report to Brigadier Catlock that he had made as thorough an investigation as was possible. The method he employed was rudimentary, but he judged that it was sufficient, as the misery of the people made it evident that they were politically innocuous: he spoke to the refugees in his bad German, and if they answered him in better, he concluded that they were Volksdeutsche and not Croats or Slovenes. Most of them replied fluently enough, although a few could barely speak German at all. The colonel did not pay much attention to that, because he knew that the Jugoslavs were classifying and expelling as Volksdeutsche persons whose Germanic ancestry was exceedingly remote.

Indeed, as he passed from compartment to compartment, the colonel soon ceased to pay much attention to what sort of German he or anybody else spoke, because of the suffering all about him and his own reactions to it. At first, as he looked at the huddled groups of women with greasy matted hair and men with dirty beards and children with lean pale faces and protruding eyes, he hated the Jugo-slavs for causing so much suffering, and then, as group succeeded group and stench and tears and hopelessness kept recurring in the same pattern, he began to hate the Volksdeutsche for suffering so much and finally even to believe that they could not really be suffering because there were so many of them suffering and they all looked alike. Perhaps, he reflected, this was what helped surgeons and torturers to do their work efficiently: the illusion that masses of people could not really suffer, but only ones and twos and threes.

He knew that he was wrong, of course, and he had argued himself back into his original pity by the time that he had reached the last carriage in the train. There, as he watched a mother with a bruised and swollen face trying to comfort her baby while her small girl of nine sat staring in front of her with patient hopelessness, he told himself that cruelty was the greatest of all sins, the ultimately shaming and shocking thing, and that lesser sins were sins only in so far as they contributed to or produced cruelty. No progress, he decided, could be made towards real peace until men had been persuaded that it was a

153

crime to be cruel, not only to those they could not see, but also to those they could see.

When he had thought that out, he began to feel superior to Reverend Mother Auxilia and her nuns, because they were righteous by rubric while he was trying to hammer out a new code by which all men could achieve happiness. Then he asked himself if he would give up his bed readily to the mother and her children and knew almost at once that he would grumble about it and try to find excuses for not doing so, whereas the nuns would give up theirs with a smile and would pray all night in the chapel in thanksgiving for having been privileged to shelter Christ hungering in the person of His creatures. Colonel Nicobar no longer knew what he thought when he got out onto the platform again and began to walk back towards where he thought Schwester Kasimira and Schwester Michaela might be.

He found them more easily than he had expected, running towards him with excited faces.

'Herr Oberst, Herr Oberst, Maria Bühlen's on the train and you didn't recognize her, but she recognized you,' Schwester Kasimira said.

'Herr Oberst, she escaped from the Russian train when it was going through Hungary and, after many saddest but oh so wonderful adventures, she managed to get on this train, because somebody was telling her that it was coming to Vienna,' Schwester Michaela said.

'Bitte schön, Herr Oberst, now you will not be handing her back to the Russians,' Schwester Kasimira said.

'Our Lord has worked a miracle, sending us to the station like this to meet her,' Schwester Michaela said.

'Bitte Schön, Herr Oberst, the Lord will only think out another miracle if you send her back, so it will not be worth while,' Schwester Kasimira said.

'And then she is so very beautiful, although of course she is tired now, but she will look beautiful again when she has slept herself awake,' Schwester Michaela said.

Down at the far end of the train somebody began to sing *Stille Nacht, Heilige Nacht*. The hymn rose in hope and fell in blessing upon the snow and the empty starless night and the three dead men lying on the platform and the priest walking up and down. A little girl of five or six was also walking up and down the platform now, with her mother holding her hand, and the sound of the hymn blessed her, too, because she was a little girl at Christmas. *Stille Nacht, Heilige Nacht*. The colonel turned away from the mystery of suffering to the eager, enquiring faces of the nuns.

'There will no longer be any need to send Maria Bühlen back to Russia, but you must not tell Colonel Piniev that she is here again,' he said. 'But I don't know how we're going to get her out of the station.'

'God will find a way,' Schwester Kasimira said.

And God did, for at that moment word came through that the British had agreed to accommodate the refugees in one of their camps and, in the ensuing exodus, it was easy for the colonel and the nuns to take Maria with them.

XIII

SWITCHING ROUND IN HIS CHAIR like a naughty boy looking behind him in church, Brigadier Catlock gave Colonel Nicobar an angry glance as he entered his office, and then revolved back again to the telephone. 'No, my name is not Dolly and I do not want to buy a pair of silk stockings,' he shouted, and banged down the receiver. 'Sometimes I don't know what the army's coming to what with A.T.S. and female civilian secretaries, and welfare and being kind to soldiers,' he said to the colonel. 'Well, Hooky, what is it this time? I don't seem to remember sending for you.'

'As a matter of fact, sir, you didn't send for me, but I thought . . .'

'Ever hear the story of what thought did, Hooky? Thought missed the last bus.' The brigadier shrieked with laughter at his own wit. 'Never heard that one before, have you?'

'No, sir,' the colonel said.

'Well, you've heard it now, Hooky,' the brigadier said. 'Well, seeing you're here, perhaps you'd better carry on.'

'I *imagined*, sir, that you'd like a report on my inspection of that Jugoslav refugee train the other night,' the colonel said.

157

'Displaced Persons, Hooky; there ain't no such thing as refugees, at least so I am informed,' the brigadier said.

During his Army career, Colonel Nicobar had always regulated his relations with his superior officers on the assumption that formal respect was owed only to those holding rank two degrees superior to his own. Brigadier Catlock, however, liked yes-men, and he had to atone for not being a yes-man by doling out all the vocatives of respect he could muster, even although the brigadier wore only one more pip than himself and that extra pip represented an appointment and not a rank. As he prepared to express his irritation through the vehicle of italicized humility, the colonel reflected that one never really got to the top of the tree in the Army. When he had been a lieutenant, he had imagined that it must be grand to be a major, and when he had been a major, he had hoped all his troubles would stop when he was a colonel, and now he was a colonel, he was still treated as a dogsbody and wanted to be a major-or lieutenant-general so that he could give young Catlock a good sock in the eye.

'Displaced Persons, then, sir,' he said. 'They were all as far as I could gather, sir, Volksdeutsche.'

'And how did you gather, Hooky, how did you gather?' The brigadier wriggled about in his chair, as though trying to scratch the base of his spine. 'Go on, please; I'm beginning to be interested.'

158

The telephone rang, and he took up the receiver with a gesture of impatience. 'On the contrary, sir,' he said when he had listened for a few seconds to the crackle at the other end; 'on the contrary, sir, not only did I never utter a disparaging word about the officer in question, but as far as I know I am one of the few people who ever said anything in his favour. That's right, sir. I couldn't agree with you more. Not a clue. Ivory from the navel upwards. Of course, sir. Entirely off the record.'

He replaced the receiver with a broad, contented smile. 'You weren't meant to hear that one, Hooky,' he said. 'But strictly between you and me some of these highly paid officers get a little touchy about their dignity at times. Can't see the peace for the crossed swords. Well, what were we talking about?'

'Jug Volksdeutsche Displaced Persons, sir,' the colonel said.

'Stick them on the wall, Hooky; I don't know that I'm interested frightfully,' the brigadier said.

'But you seemed to want me to vet them as regards subversive activities, sir,' the colonel said.

'Put it in writing, Hooky,' the brigadier said.

'Certainly, sir,' the colonel said. 'And Maria Bühlen's turned up again.'

'Stick her on the wall, too, Hooky, stick them all on the wall,' the brigadier said.

'Yes, sir, but . . .' the colonel said.

159

'Then put her in writing too, Hooky, put them all in writing,' the brigadier said.

The colonel was not feeling in a particularly good mood as he walked back to the office, even although the band of the Argyll and Sutherland Highlanders was playing, skirling the nut-brown maiden over the roofs of Vienna. He cheered up, however, when he came across his new friend, the small girl who often played outside his office. In a neat little pinafore and with two frisks of diminutive black pigtail she ran towards him.

'Guten Morgen, Mickey Mouse,' the colonel greeted.

'Mickey Mouse, ha, ha.' The small girl shrieked with mirth. 'Mickey Mouse verstehe nicht. Warum Mickey Mouse?'

'Weil . . .' But the colonel's German was not good enough for him to explain to the child that he called her Mickey Mouse because she looked like Mickey Mouse, so instead he asked her the questions he knew by heart.

'Wie alt bist du?'

'Ich bin fünf jahre alt.'

'Warum bist du nicht in Schule heute?'

'Weil ich Feiertag habe.'

After that there didn't seem to be much to say, so they smiled at each other. As usual the colonel had forgotten to bring any chocolate with him, but the small girl didn't seem to mind that and put her hand in the colonel's and accompanied him to the door of his office, where she gravely said good-bye. From his window the colonel watched her run back to talk with the German prisoners, who were still removing rubble. Wishing that children never grew up, the colonel sat down at his desk to write his two memoranda for Brigadier Catlock, but first he began to read the contents of his in-basket, searching for possible thunderbolts.

'Mass rape by French denied,' he read. 'The French commander of the Army Ground Forces today denied that French Forces had committed a mass rape on German women. He had made an investigation of the charges and said that there was no mass rape of German women by French Forces. He said that the German mayor had stated that eleven hundred and ninety-eight rapes had occurred during the French occupation, whereas he believed that a thorough investigation would show only about eight hundred probable rapes.' He looked up as Sergeant Moonlight entered the room. 'Ah, Moonlight, I want a word with you,' he said. 'Private Brownlee has been complaining to me that you've been rude to her.'

'Oh, no, sir, I wasn't rude, sir; I just told her to use her loaf and shake the fog out of er ead,' Sergeant Moonlight said.

The colonel laughed.

'I see,' he said. 'Well, perhaps you could have expressed your discontent a little more delicately. Girls are a bit more sensitive than men, you know.' Having delivered this shadow of a rebuke, he changed the subject at once. 'Well, Moonlight, and how do you like Vienna?' he asked.

'Not a patch on Brixton, sir,' Sergeant Moonlight said. 'Beer ain't no good.'

'But don't you get any wine in the sergeants' mess?' the colonel asked.

'Wine's a downfall drink,' Sergeant Moonlight said.

The colonel smiled, knowing the superstition of the troops.

'And dancing?' he asked. 'Get any dancing?'

'In the sweat box, sir,' Sergeant Moonlight said. 'I don't mind doing a bit of fratting myself, sir, but I prefer my Fräuleins in the open air.'

The colonel knew that the sergeant did, for one night, walking home from dining with Brigadier Catlock, he had seen the sergeant, caught up in a clumsy embrace in a doorway, with a blowsy blonde in a squeegee hat. He had concluded that both participants looked too ugly for their pleasure to be sinful. He had hoped that God would see things that way, too, and be merciful to His creatures, who, in a lonely world of tramlines, sometimes caricatured the gestures of tenderness.

'Well, Moonlight, don't get yourself into trouble,' he said, and went on reading his way through the abracadabra in his in-basket.

162

XIV

Smoothing out the pleats of his Black Watch kilt, Twingo drew his chest up against his bright new medal ribbons and pirouetted in front of Senior Sub-altern Quail.

'Am I looking operational?' he asked.

Audrey nodded.

'Smashing,' she said. 'Going out in a big way?'

'With trumpets and banners,' Twingo said.

'With Maria, I suppose?' Audrey asked.

'I'm afraid so, my dear, but there's nothing to flap about,' Twingo said. 'She doesn't strike me as being frightfully interested.'

'I wish I could think so,' Audrey said. 'Sorry, Twingo, that's a rotten thing to say. Well, I hope you don't get caught gate-crashing frat into Sacher's.' She managed to smile and hoped the wobbling she felt inside her wasn't showing on her lips. Then she walked away to change, so that she wouldn't be there to see Maria coming down in the frock which Schwester Michaela was supposed to have lent her.

Colonel Nicobar was there, however, and he stood with Twingo in the hall and watched the girl walk slowly downstairs with Schwester Kasimira on one side of her and Schwester Michaela on the other. Her hair was very gold against the nuns' black veils and the fountain of her frock flashed about her feet in a swift pale blue spray. The colonel remembered when he had been young and had waited for beautiful girls to come downstairs. It seemed like yesterday and yet it was a long time ago.

'She's very lovely, isn't she?' Schwester Michaela said.

'She is also good and that is what is more important,' Schwester Kasimira said. 'Reverend Mother thinks that she is very good. We are all thinking that she is very good.'

The girl did not know how to answer those compliments and they all stood around the door in one of those self-conscious groups whose members hesitate to separate for fear of appearing too anxious to do so. The two nuns smiled benignly and made small unnecessary motions with their hands, and the girl kept her gaze lowered because she didn't like being looked at so much, and the colonel tried to look at the nuns instead of at the girl, whose youth made him feel old. Twingo was in an itch to be off, but was too shy to take the initiative. The gaiety of the girl's frock and the colonel's red tabs was sobered by the wisdom of the nuns' habits.

'Reverend Mother let me be keeping that dress when I am become a nun, but of course I am not to be taking it out and looking at it,' Schwester Mi-

164

chaela said. 'But Maria has also dresses of her own, of course.'

'But none that are quite so pretty,' Maria said.

'It is not necessarily sinful to wear pretty dresses,' Schwester Kasimira said. 'It is the intention with which they are worn that matters.'

'Perhaps we'd better be going,' Twingo said at last.

They went, before a discussion on the supernatural aspects of titivation could begin. In the car on the way to Sacher's, Twingo explained to the girl that she must on no account speak while he was obtaining the tickets for dinner at the reception desk, as it was forbidden to invite or to dine there girls who did not belong to one of the four Allied military organizations. He said that, ordinarily speaking, he did not take Austrian girls out to dinner, but that he had considered himself justified in making an exception in her case. Anyway, he thought that it was a stupid rule, as it prevented British officers getting to know the Austrians well, and it made the British girls too cocksure because like that they had no competition and could get a date with a different man every day of the week, no matter how ugly they were. To all this the girl answered nothing, sitting back in her corner with her hands folded in her lap and not looking at him at all. He thought, therefore, that she had not understood, and, as he was anxious that she should not betray her nationality at the reception desk, he began to explain all over again, but when he said that he never took Austrian girls out, she interrupted him.

'Why do you speak to me about Austrian girls?' she asked. 'Ich bin nicht Austrian girl. Ich bin Volksdeutsches Mädchen, Russisches Volksdeutsches Mädchen, Alliertes Russisches Volksdeutsches Mädchen, Allied Russian Volksdeutsche girl; so please do not be speaking to me again about Austrian girls.'

'But, Maria,' Twingo said.

'Please do not be calling me "Maria," ' she said. 'You would not be calling one of your English girls "Maria" after you had been knowing her since only five minutes. An Austrian girl, perhaps, but not an English girl. I am not an Austrian girl. I am a Volksdeutsches girl. So please do not be calling me "Maria" because I do not like it and my name is Fräulein Bühlen.'

'Oh dear,' Twingo said under his breath, but aloud he said: 'Certainly, Fräulein Bühlen, if that is your wish.'

'It is my wish, Herr Major,' the girl said. 'And if you are afraid to be taking me out to dinner in one of your military restaurants, then please to tell the driver, presto subito to be driving back to the convent,' she said.

'Of course I am not afraid,' Twingo said.

It had always been the same way, he reflected, as they drove on in silence: Cynthia, whom he had

courted for three years, had married that little
shocker in plus fours with the motor bicycle; Sally
with the red hair, and Eileen with the fair, they had
both given him the go-by too; Audrey, whom he
didn't love, seemed to be the only one who had suc-
cumbed. His misery was still enduring when they
drove up at Sacher's and helped him to pass the
reception desk without nervousness. He chose a
table in the furthermost room, where they would be
least likely to be remarked.

Observing her at leisure while she was choosing
what she was going to eat, he noticed with relief that
she was not quite so beautiful as he had at first
imagined her to be, because beautiful women had
always made him frightened and tongue-tied. Her
cheekbones were a little too prominent, he thought,
and her hair was too flaxen and German and brushed
down in the middle. He was beginning to hope that
her ankles were thicker than he had thought when
she turned to him with large grey sorrowful eyes
which lighted the solemnity of her face to loveliness
and made him afraid of her again.

'I am thinking that I have been a pig to you,' she
said.

'Of course not,' Twingo said. 'I was stupid and
put my foot in it and you were perfectly right to be
a pig to me, but of course you weren't a pig to me.
Waiter, two sherries.'

'I am also thinking that I must ask your pardon,'

she said, stretching her hand across the table and laying it gently on his. 'You will please to forgive me when I am reminding you that I have lately been through very many unpleasant experiences. You will please to remember that I am very tired and unhappy.'

'Of course, of course, but there's nothing to forgive,' Twingo said. What an ass he'd been, talking about the difficulty of wangling past a reception desk to a girl who had just escaped from being forcibly repatriated by the Russians! And she had never, as far as he knew, said a word about her experiences. 'Ich bin zurückgekommen, I have come back because I did not wish to return to Russia,' was all that Schwester Kasimira said that she had said. Before the war Twingo had always refrained from reading Edgar Wallace on the ground that his novels bore no resemblance to life, but now life in Central Europe was all Edgar Wallace, with ordinary young girls doing all sorts of brave deeds and comfortable things gone for ever.

'But you no longer need to be afraid,' he said. 'The fact that you are a Volksdeutscher means that you do not need to go back to Russia. The colonel is quite sure of that now. It was all a mistake in the first instance, but it was not the colonel's fault. He was only obeying orders; but now he is no longer under any obligation to send you back and he will not do so.'

'Even if the Russians are knowing that I am here and are asking for me, he will not send me back? You are sure of that?' she asked.

'Of course I am sure of that,' he said.

She smiled at him. Her teeth were very young and her tongue between them was young too.

'I am thinking that you may be calling me Maria, presto subito, if you like,' she said.

'Thank you,' he said. 'But tell me: why do you always say presto subito?'

'It is the foolish Italian I used to talk when I was dancing in Milan,' she said. 'I can talk a little French, too, but not very good. I am sorry that I was being rude to you in the car just now and you must forgive me, but I am not altogether liking the Austrian people who are one day Nazis, and then the next day, when the Allies come, it is all a mistake and none of them were ever Nazis. And so I am not pleased when you are calling me an Austrian girl, because I am a Russian Volksdeutscher and I am proud of being a Russian Volksdeutscher.'

'And yet you do not wish to go back to Russia?' Twingo asked.

'A girl can be proud of being a Russian without being a communist,' she said. She was silent while the waiter placed their two glasses of sherry on the table and then she went on again. 'Why is it that you English people are not understanding political hatred?' she asked.

169

'Indifference, perhaps,' Twingo said. 'Or the translation of the Bible into English, or fair play, or an ordinary decent humble understanding that there may be something to be said for the other chap's point of view.'

'What an awful lot of things and I am not understanding any of them!' she said. 'Perhaps it is because you speak too fast or perhaps it is because you think too slow. Anyway, I do not know. But I am unable not to hate about politics, and the world is all about politics nowadays, and I must hate those who are not thinking that my kind of politics is right. Once the world was about religion, but I am not thinking that the world is very much about religion today, although when I am praying I am hoping that it is a little about religion, because I am wanting to go to heaven when I die. When I am praying with the nuns in their chapel, I believe that the world is greatly about religion, but when I am coming back into the streets again and seeing hungry men and women, I am not greatly believing that the world is very much about religion. When I was in that train coming back from Hungary, I was not believing that the world was greatly about religion. And when I was on the train going back to Russia, I was sure that the world was not at all about religion. But we shall not talk about these things because they make me sad and perhaps they will make you sad also, who do not think much about politics, because the Bible has been translated into English. I think about politics, because I believe very much in my own kind of politics, which I think will make all the people in the world happy, and I hate those who have another kind of politics, because I am thinking that their kind of politics will be making all the people in the world sad.'

Twingo thought of the girls he knew in England whose politics were clothing coupons. Even those who had served in the war had never really known the difference between fascism and communism or been able to define their ideology. And not only the girls, the men as well, as all those dreadful instructional articles in the service press before the general election had proved. That, of course, was the worst of the via media: it fired nobody except its opponents and fanaticism was the only thing which could save the world in spite of what the journalists said.

'I say, tell me more,' he said.

She shook her head.

'I have said that I did not wish to talk about these things because they are making me sad,' she said.

'Tell me about your escape from the Russians, then,' he said. 'Was it fearfully exciting?'

'I am not wishing to talk about that either, because that also would make me sad,' she said. 'Let us talk about something gay, and please not to be looking hurt, because I am liking you a lot.'

171

'I like you, too,' Twingo said.

The couple at the next table didn't seem to be talking about politics either. With their hands locked beneath the table, they mooned meatily into each other's eyes.

'Holding hands like nobody's business,' Twingo said.

'"Like nobody's business"?' Maria asked. 'Once again I am afraid that I am not understanding.'

Twingo explained.

XV

THE COLONEL'S GERMAN was coming along nicely and he was able to explain, more or less in her own tongue to Reverend Mother Auxilia, just how the English made tea. 'Das ist nicht sehr schwer,' he said, brandishing an empty tea pot above the sink in the scullery. 'Im Gegenteil ist es sehr leicht. Erst müssen Sie ein wenig heisses Wasser in die Teekanne stecken aber ohne Tee, die man noch nicht braucht. Dann müssen Sie so mit der Teekanne machen, skirrywirrywirry, und dann das heisse Wasser auswerfen. Dann müssen Sie einen Löffel Tee für jede Persone in die Teekanne stecken und einen Löffel Tee für die Teekanne selbst. Die Ausländer können nie Tee sondern nur Kaffee machen,' he concluded.

'So that's the form, is it?' Reverend Mother Auxilia asked, whose Army English was coming along nicely too.

'That's the form,' the colonel said. 'Personally, I'm not very fond of tea, although I'm supposed to be an Englishman.'

'Sometimes, Herr Oberst, you do not seem to me to be very fond of your fellow-countrymen either,' Reverend Mother Auxilia said.

173

'On the contrary, I've always been very fond of the English: in fact, I don't mind them at all,' the colonel said. 'Perhaps the trouble with me is that like you and Edith Cavell I do not believe that patriotism is enough. In fact, not only is it not enough, but at times it is even highly dangerous, because one country's only got to be overpatriotic for the rest to be obliged to be overpatriotic back. No, a sane universalism's the only cure, but how you're going to get that into the thick skulls of men beats me. Now, don't start arguing religion at me, Reverend Mother, because it's no use; currency as well as creed has got to come in it. Well, let's go back to the parlour now that I have explained to you how the English make tea.'

The colonel and Reverend Mother Auxilia sat together in the parlour most evenings now, because Twingo was often out with Maria and Audrey was usually out to dine too, as Colonel Omicron was by no means the only officer in Vienna who was anxious to share her society. Tonight, however, they found Schwester Kasimira waiting for them, her big damp splotchy face alight with excitement.

'Oh, Reverend Mother, you will never guess!' she exclaimed. 'But this evening the most wonderful of all things has happened. Franz has come back from Russia. He has been a prisoner, but he has been released. My brother, you know. Oh, but I am so

174

very glad and I am sure, Reverend Mother, that you will be glad too, because you know how much I have been wanting this, and you, Herr Oberst, you must be glad too. Bitte schön, Reverend Mother, that I may bring him in here, that he may speak to you and tell you how glad he is to have been sent home from Russia.'

'But certainly, Schwester Kasimira,' Reverend Mother said. 'I shall be only too pleased to speak to him. And you know that I am glad that he has come back. And I am sure that the Herr Oberst is very glad too.'

The colonel made a polite noise. He was glad, of course, for Schwester Kasimira's sake that her brother had come back from Russia, but he couldn't feel jubilant about the fact, even although he knew how much it pleased Schwester Kasimira. He supposed that in order to feel really glad one would require to be either Schwester Kasimira or her brother. Especially her brother. A really terrible war that must have been, with the cold and the snow and not enough food and getting rifle-butted about by the Russians when you were taken prisoner. He ought to be feeling very glad for Schwester Kasimira's sake that her brother had come back from Russia, but, to be quite honest with himself, he was feeling a little bit annoyed with him for having come back this particular evening and spoiled his tête-a-tête with Reverend Mother Auxilia, with whom he had been hoping to discuss, comfortably, the rotten state of the world. How glad, then, was he?

Deliberately the colonel set himself to assess his sentiment. Would he have given a packet of cigarettes in order that Schwester Kasimira's brother might be released from Russia? Yes, certainly he would have given a packet of cigarettes, two packets even, three even. Would he have given a week's N.A.A.F.I. ration? Less certainly, grumblingly, using a spark of alliterative earthy words, he would have given a week's N.A.A.F.I. ration. Ten pounds? More readily than the week's N.A.A.F.I. ration, because they would not be so difficult to replace. A hundred pounds? Well, it was all very well, but Schwester Kasimira must understand that he had a wife and two daughters to support. He brushed away the dishonest excuse. He would have given either a week's N.A.A.F.I. ration or ten pounds and not a cigarette or a penny more to spare Schwester Kasimira's brother the discomfort and the privations which he must have endured as a prisoner of war in Russia, and he would have given neither of them without grumbling and wishing to hell that he wasn't forced to make the sacrifice.

These, then, were the limits to his charity, the virtue whose practice alone could save the world from destruction. Could the world be saved from destruction by ten pounds or a week's N.A.A.F.I. ration, even when sacrificed by eighteen hundred thousand million human beings? The answer was, of course, that the world could not be saved from destruction by ten pounds or a week's N.A.A.F.I. ration, even when sacrificed by eighteen hundred thousand million human beings.

The knowledge that the world was not going to be saved from destruction made him miserable, but the knowledge of his own guilt in the matter made him more miserable still. Reverend Mother Auxilia had once said to him that people's own faults were precisely those which they hated most when they discovered them in others, and he, who had been expecting Brazil and Soviet Russia to sacrifice their exports for the welfare of Belgium and Albania, wouldn't give up more than ten pounds of his ease to succour a fellow human being. He was beginning to realize how much he would dislike meeting another man exactly like himself when Schwester Kasimira came back with her brother, whom she led by the hand.

Schwester Kasimira's brother walked with a stick and limped badly. He was wearing a civilian suit made of inferior tweed. His face was drawn and thin and his eyes were large and unhappy. He appeared to be about forty years of age, but the colonel thought that it was possible that the lines on his face made him look older than he really was. His hair was thin, going grey at the temples. He drew himself to attention.

'Buchardt, Oberst-Leutnant,' he announced, and, turning to the colonel, bowed slightly and said in English: 'But perhaps I have no longer any right so to style myself. A beaten soldier is no longer a soldier, no?'

'A good soldier is always a soldier, Herr Oberst-leutnant,' the colonel said as he shook hands after Reverend Mother Auxilia. Ashamed of being neatly dressed in uniform, when Schwester Kasimira's brother was so poorly clad, he did his best to put the other at ease. 'Ich höre, dass Sie in Russland gekämpft haben,' he said in his best German.

Schwester Kasimira's brother bowed again.

'Schwerer Kampf,' he said.

The colonel tried to think up something else to say about the campaign in Russia, but even in English he could find nothing. Minsk, Orel, Kiev, Odessa, what could he say about them that would not be insulting to the other, who had lost the war? He decided to say something about how unpleasant it must have been to fight in all that snow and was trying to think out the words in German when Schwester Kasimira said:

'My brother says that the Russians were not so unkind to him after all.'

'I am glad that the Russians were kind to you,' Reverend Mother Auxilia said.

'I did not say that they were kind,' Herr Buchardt said. 'The Russians are never kind to prisoners of war.' He stopped. 'Die Russen ... But it is better not to discuss them.'

Colonel Nicobar suddenly realized that both Reverend Mother Auxilia and Schwester Kasimira must have wanted Germany to win the war. As Austrians, they must have wanted Germany to win. As Christians, they must have wanted Germany to win, because for them Stalin must have been so obviously anti-Christ and communism a very real bogey, in spite of the optimism of British Broadcasting Corporation announcers. Perhaps Pope Pius the Twelfth himself had been wanting Germany to win. Perhaps His Holiness still wished that Germany had won. It must be difficult for a Latin mind, even when illumined by the Holy Ghost, to accept hordes of non-practising Presbyterian Highlanders, copulating G.I.s, and predatory Russians as more adequately defending Christian civilisation than the millions of Catholics who had fought against them. And yet, Russia and jingoism apart, the colonel was convinced that this was indeed the case, although he didn't know quite how to explain it to Reverend Mother Auxilia and Schwester Kasimira, without hurting their feelings or seeming to claim too much for Britain and America. There was a clean wind blowing in both these countries which was blowing in no other, certainly not in Italy and in Spain. Perhaps, though, as a Catholic padre had once suggested to him, the Italians would have been even

179

more ignoble if they had been Methodists. And probably the Pope hadn't taken sides at all, sorrowing only over the new rent in Christ's garment. The Japanese, though. The Pope couldn't possibly have wanted the Japs to win. Faced by the charity of three of his ex-enemies talking his own language between themselves in order that he should understand every word they said, the colonel did not know what to think.

'In all groups and assemblies of men there are good and there are bad men,' he said. 'It is unprofitable to generalize. There are good Russians and bad Russians just as there are good Germans and bad Germans and good Englishmen and bad Englishmen,' he said. Afraid that what he said must sound trite, he sought refuge in obscurity. 'I mean that the distribution of what Reverend Mother Auxilia would call the grace of God cannot be charted geographically.'

'All that is obvious,' Herr Buchardt said, a little rudely, the colonel thought. 'Common men all over the world understand that but their leaders do not, or if their leaders do, they do not say so. Common men all over the world wish only to live in moderate comfort with their families, but they do not know how to choose leaders who understand this. It is the leaders of the world who are at fault, for instead of leading they mislead.'

'That is perhaps an oversimplification,' the colonel

said. 'If the Lord God had really wanted there to be no wars, He ought to have made a world consisting of one continent surrounded by one ocean. On that continent there should have been no natural barriers and all men should have spoken one language.'

'And the men who lived on that island ought to have been able to live without food,' Herr Buchardt said.

'Really, when one comes to think of it, the Lord God oughtn't to have created man at all,' the colonel said. 'I believe that was one of the major pronouncements ever made by that Delphic gas bag Marie Corelli, although I don't suppose you've ever heard of her.' He suddenly realized that he oughtn't to be talking like this in front of the nuns. 'I'm sorry, Reverend Mother,' he said.

'Almighty God created man to honour Him, to obey Him, and to serve Him, Franz,' Schwester Kasimira said. 'It is not for us to question the wisdom of His acts.' It was obvious from the glow in her eyes that there was much else she wished to say, but the colonel saw that the proper words weren't going to come even to her, however much she believed.

'When men are freezing to death on the plains of Russia, they are bound to question the wisdom of His acts,' Herr Buchardt said.

'They would perhaps be better occupied in questioning the wisdom of their own folly,' Reverend

Mother Auxilia said. 'I do not wish to appear unsympathetic, but all man's miseries come from his initial rebellion against God.'

'The Garden of Eden,' Herr Buchardt sneered. 'Talk about that to men who are dying in the snow in Russia, speak about Eve and apples to men as the shells are rushing through the woods and there are fires everywhere! Listen and I shall tell you something. When Hitler and Goebbels were telling us that the war against Russia was a holy war against communism, what was the Church saying? What was the Pope in Rome doing? Did he ever say whether the war against Russia was a holy war or not? No, he did not tell the Germans and the Austrians whether the war against Russia was holy or not any more than he told the British that the war against Germany was holy. And what were the German priests saying? Some of them were saying that it was a holy war and others were not so sure, but all of them were saying that it was a sin for a man to drink too much wine or to make love to a pretty girl if he was not married to her.

'Well, when a man is in a battle and a priest comes to comfort him before he is killed, he wants to be told other things than that it is a sin to drink too much wine or for him to make love to a pretty girl if he is not married to her. A man who is going to be killed in battle needs to drink too much wine and to make love to pretty girls. What is more, all through the

182

ages the good soldier, the brave fighter, has not been the man who was good at saying his prayers in churches, but rather he has been the man who was good at drinking wine and making love to pretty girls. But what he wants to know before he is killed in the snow is why those who are good at saying their prayers in churches want him to try to kill other men who are good at drinking wine and making love to pretty girls. He wants to know who is right and who is wrong and why he must suffer and make other men suffer these so terrible sore things.

'Please do not be misunderstanding me. The soldier who fights and drinks too much wine and makes love to pretty girls is an unhappy man, and he likes Jesus Christ and all that He has said, but he often is not liking very much those who say that they speak in His Name.' He looked appealingly at both the nuns, but especially did he look at his sister, who was staring at him with damp misery. 'Please not to be hurt by what I have just said. Please to be understanding that the young men who fight your wars for you and then are forgotten are not wicked. They are wanting to hear a voice, that is all; but they are wanting to hear a voice which they can understand and not big cold words which sound grandly in cathedrals. They are still wanting to hear it, before it is too late, and before their sons have got to go and be wounded and die at night on the open plains.'

'Oh, Franz, I am so very sorry that you are thinking these terrible things,' Schwester Kasimira said.

'Please believe that I am very serious about what I say,' Herr Buchardt said. 'And not only for myself, but for thousands of others. When we were fighting the war we were told that we were doing right, but now that we have lost it, we are told that we have been doing wrong. We are wanting to know why.'

'The question is not entirely theological,' the colonel said and quoted:

For it's Tommy this, an' Tommy that, an' 'Chuck him out, the brute!'
But it's 'Saviour of 'is country' when the guns begin to shoot.

'On the contrary, the question is entirely theological,' Reverend Mother began. 'Ingratitude is a sin like any other sin.'

'And as for all the other things you have said, I am afraid I am not clever enough to reply, but of course there's an answer, because the Lord couldn't let there not be an answer,' Schwester Kasimira said.

'The answer is in each man's heart as he turns his back on sanctifying grace and says, "This I shall be doing because others are doing it" and "That I shall not be doing because nobody else is doing it,"' Reverend Mother Auxilia said.

XVI

THEY WALKED IN LOVE in a pale green world through the trees, with moonbeams splintering at their feet. The chapel windows were lighted, and the stained-glass robes of Saint Walburga of Graz shone in a big red blob, because it was *Quarant' Ore* and the nuns were praying specially hard. They stopped in a lonely place. Twingo ran his arms round Maria's waist under her coat and kissed her beneath her wide hat.

'It's all right, my sweet,' he said.

'It is all right when I am being with you,' she said.

'Oh, my sweet, my sweet, my lovely girl and your funny little ears and your soft hair and your legs that are friendly when you go upstairs,' Twingo said.

'I am afraid sometimes that I am not being very beautiful for you,' she said.

'Maria darling, you're the most beautiful thing that I have ever seen,' Twingo said. 'I shall always be wanting to kiss you, Maria,' he said. 'O God, I love you, Maria, I adore you, oh, whee!'

He caught her to him, pushing her hair back from her forehead. She stood and let herself be kissed.

Sometimes she kissed him back, but now she stood there, with her face pale, letting him love her.

'Say something to me in German,' he said.

'Ich habe dich gern,' she said.

'And in Russian,' he said.

She made swift sounds which he did not understand.

'And in German again,' he said.

'Du bist ein heisser Mann,' she said, and pushed him away a little.

'Look here, Maria, don't get things wrong,' Twingo said. 'I know what you're thinking. I've done the same things to other girls in the past, of course, but I've never done them the same way as I'm doing them to you.'

'I think that I am believing that, Twingo,' she said, still with her arms at her sides.

'This is the spirit as well as the body, Maria,' Twingo said.

'I think that I am believing that also,' she said.

'I know that it is the spirit as well as the body because I am happy when I see you in the morning and because I am sad when I think of this garden without you in it and because I feel humble when I see you so lovely,' Twingo said.

'Then, if you love me with your spirit as well as with your body, you may be touching me,' she said.

'I'm afraid I'm a little rough,' he said.

'Macht nichts,' she said.

186

'I'm only rough because I love you,' he said.

'I am glad that you think that I am being beautiful enough for you,' she said.

'I love you so much that I even love your handwriting,' he said.

'I am being glad of that,' she said. 'You will be seeing more of it soon.'

'Soon?' Twingo asked.

'Presto subito,' she said, stroking his hair. 'Listen, Twingo: I am wanting you to be sensible. I am also wanting you to help me. I cannot continue to live in the convent with the Russians looking for me. I cannot go on living in Vienna with the Russians looking for me. I am knowing that Colonel Nicobar will not be sending me back, of course, but I am also knowing that it is the right of the Russians to send back their own citizens from Vienna.'

'But you're a Volksdeutscher,' Twingo said.

'A Russian Volksdeutscher,' Maria said.

'Then what do you want to do?' he asked.

'I want you to ask Colonel Nicobar to arrange for me to be sent down to the British Zone of Austria,' she said. 'Oh, I know it is not permitted, but you are not knowing how great the danger is for me and how frightened I am when I am waking up at nights and thinking that I may still be sent back to Russia. Please, Twingo. I am being so frightened when I am not with you and sometimes I am not thinking that you understand.'

'Of course I understand, Maria,' Twingo said. 'And of course I'll ask Colonel Nicobar and of course he'll say yes and I'll come down and see you every week-end. I'm afraid you must think me a selfish brute for not understanding.'

'Macht nichts,' she said.

'I think I should die if anything happened to you, Maria,' he said.

'When I am with you like this, I am feeling that nothing can happen to me again,' she said.

'Dear sweet Maria: I'm afraid I'm going to be rough again,' he said.

'Macht nichts,' she said.

XVII

THE NUNS WERE ARGUING among themselves
about how they thought Colonel Nicobar's left arm
would be resurrected from the dead, the real one
which he had lost on the Menin Road. The colonel
had told them that it had been burned, but Schwester
Kasimira didn't think the colonel could be considered guilty of the sin of cremation as he himself
hadn't given orders for it to be burned, and anyway,
an arm could scarcely be considered the temple of
the Holy Ghost, although it was just possible that
Almighty God might have allowed a little Paraclete
to seep in.

That, however, was not the point. The point
was where would the colonel's left arm wait to join
the colonel's glorified body when, after the general
judgment, the latter would go, as the nuns hoped,
to live for ever with the Lord Jesus Christ in heaven.

Schwester Kasimira said that she thought that
there was a special limbo where burnt bodies went,
there to await rejunction to their souls when the last
trump sounded, but Schwester Michaela said that
was silly and that burnt bodies became carbonic-
acid gas and didn't need a special limbo. 'Modus
quo corporibus adhaerent spiritus comprehendi ab

189

hominibus non potest et hoc tamen homo est,' Reverend Mother Auxilia said, quoting Saint Augustine to put an end to their chattering, and pointed out that our Lord could raise carbonic-acid gas as well as bodies from the dead, since He was God.

The colonel, who was listening to the discussion, said that he could answer about his artificial arm all right, as that belonged to the British Government, and the Ministry of Pensions would send round to collect it as soon as he died, but the nuns did not smile much.

Schwester Kasimira then said that her brother was coming that evening and that she would be grateful if the colonel would entertain him, as next day was Saint Joseph's day and she had a lot of work to do in the chapel, putting flowers on the altar and laying out the vestments in the sacristy. So the colonel went back into his anteroom and sat down to read the papers while awaiting the arrival of Herr Buchardt. The news was not exhilarating, as victory did not appear to have brought either peace or plenty to the world, but there was an article on 'Can Love Survive in a Flat?' by a leading larynxologist. Then Herr Buchardt arrived, looking, as usual, pale and worn. The colonel offered his visitor a drink, which he accepted, and the two sat down opposite each other.

'Your sister asks me to make her excuses to you,'

190

the colonel said. 'She is busy in the chapel, as to-morrow is a feast day.'

Herr Buchardt nodded, but said nothing.

'You are now out of the army for good, I suppose,' the colonel said.

'As you say, I am out of the army for good, but I am also out of the army for bad,' Herr Buchardt said. 'You see, all my life I have been a soldier and I have no other profession. I am not knowing very well how I am going to earn my living. Things are not easy in Austria.'

'You said that you fought in Russia?' the colonel asked.

'In Russia and in France,' Herr Buchardt said. 'I was wounded at Sedan in 1940.'

'I was in France in 1940 too,' the colonel said.

'I did my real fighting in the last war,' Herr Buchardt said. 'I was at La Bassée in 1916 and again in 1918.'

'I was also at La Bassée in 1918,' the colonel said. 'We went into the trenches in front of Cambrin, you know, up the road from Noeux-les-Mines. First we took Auchy-la-Bassée. With a cyclist battalion, of all things. I remember standing in the trenches there and a German airman flying in low and strafing us with explosive bullets. I was very angry with that airman.'

'I, too, was often being angry with British airmen,' Herr Buchardt said.

191

'If you were at La Bassée in 1918, then perhaps you were also at Tournai in 1918, just before it all ended,' the colonel said.

'I was also at Tournai in 1918,' Herr Buchardt said.

They both sat thinking about how many times it had been their duty to kill each other. Colonel Nicobar found it easier to be amused about it having been their duty to kill each other during the earlier war than during the one which had just ended. He remembered Tournai so well, the Scheldt, the German Observation Post on the tower of the cathedral. He had had no business to be there, of course, because he had already lost his arm, but he had managed to persuade the authorities to let him go out again, not because he liked danger, but because he couldn't stand the civilians at home.

Civilians. That was what he and Buchardt ought to be talking about, the bloodiness of business men keeping the home fires burning, though their hearts were yearning. Civilians, who always let soldiers down, that's what they ought to be talking about, and politicians, who had unleashed them at each others' throats, and all the high corruption of society. Yet this war hadn't been quite the same, because the civilians had taken a packet everywhere and right seemed a little easier to distinguish from wrong, and there had been the Gestapo, although that hadn't been the fault of Herr Oberst-Leutnant

Buchardt, who had only done his duty as a soldier, he was sure.

He wanted to say something to Herr Buchardt about how extraordinary it was that they should be sitting here drinking together in spite of their having fought on opposite sides in two world wars, but he couldn't find words which wouldn't sound trite. So they both sat there in silence, thinking away behind their faces, united more by the compulsions of their calling than they were separated by the remembrance of their enmities.

'Do you remember a little village outside Tournai called La Bruyelle?' the colonel asked at length. 'One of our companies had its H.Q. there. I was on the staff then, of course, because I couldn't very well do any fighting with my left arm off, but they used to allow me to go up the line from time to time on special missions. One day the battalion commander of the company concerned sent back word to Brigade Headquarters that there was an old Belgian woman believed to be a spy in a cellar of one of the houses in the village and that they had heard her talking at night. As I was supposed to speak tolerable French, I was sent up to interrogate her, but, as the approach to the house was under enemy observation by daylight, we had to wait for nightfall. A sergeant and a company commander were to accompany me, but every minute the approach to the house was sprayed by machine-gun fire, so we had

193

to wait until a burst of fire had ended before starting out.

'We had about fifty yards to go, and I was for all running across, but the company commander and the sergeant would insist on walking and, of course, I had to walk too. We got over just before the next burst of machine-gun fire started and I can tell you I was very frightened. And then there turned out to be no old woman in the cellar after all, but only the wind moaning, and then we had to go back again, and of course the company commander and the sergeant insisted on walking again.'

His story had not been exciting, he knew, but it had been told to put his visitor at ease, and he was surprised to find Herr Buchardt paying no attention at all, but staring towards the doorway. He soon understood why, however, because Colonel Piniev was standing there, buttoned tightly into his high-necked tunic and saluting.

'This is Herr Buchardt, the brother of one of the nuns,' Colonel Nicobar said when he and the Russian colonel had greeted one another, but Colonel Piniev bowed only very slightly and did not shake hands, but went on standing with his hat with the red star on it held upside down in front of him. He was looking, Colonel Nicobar thought, more tired than when he had last seen him, with the lines running in deeper webs out from his eyes and his complexion paler than before. Colonel Nicobar wondered what caused those lines, overwork or fear of a Russian general bawling threats of Siberia. But perhaps Russian generals didn't bawl threats of Siberia. That was just the hell of it: one didn't know anything about Russian generals or what they bawled threats about or whether they bawled threats at all. One only imagined and one looked at the weariness on the faces of decent chaps like Colonel Piniev and one went on imagining.

'Maria Bühlen,' Colonel Piniev said. 'I am not saying that she is here, but I have come to ask whether she is here.'

'Maria Bühlen is not here; that's the answer to that one,' Colonel Nicobar said, and waited in fright for Colonel Piniev to ask the question which would put him in a quandary.

Three days ago, at Twingo's request, he had made arrangements for the girl to be sent down to the British Zone of Austria, where she was staying with friends of Reverend Mother Auxilia, near the Millstätter See in Carinthia. This procedure had been, as the colonel knew, irregular, because it was the province of the Russians to repatriate their own citizens from Vienna, especially those resident in the Innerestadt, which they governed equally with the three other Powers. He had been a party to it, however, because Brigadier Catlock had told him that Soviet Volksdeutsche who did not wish to return to Russia need not be compelled to do so and because his heart had been touched by the girl's plight, whose circumstances had been made so clear to him by Twingo.

'I am understanding that Maria Bühlen came back to Vienna on a train of Volksdeutsche expelled from Jugoslavia,' Colonel Piniev went on. 'I am also understanding that you and two of the nuns went to Aspang Station to meet that train.'

'Your understanding is correct,' Colonel Nicobar said. 'I went down on the express instructions of my brigadier to inspect the train from a security point of view; the two nuns came with me, because they wanted to perform works of mercy. One o'clock in the morning. I can tell you that I was not particularly pleased.'

'I am seeing that generals are difficult in all armies,' Colonel Piniev said. 'If I am here, it is because my general has asked me to come to ask you if Maria Bühlen is again in this convent, but as you are telling me that she is not again in this convent, I am thinking that I have no more questions to ask.'

Colonel Nicobar wondered why the Russian colonel didn't ask whether the girl had ever been in the convent since the arrival of the Jugoslav Volksdeutsche train in Vienna. But perhaps Colonel Piniev had been ordered to catch the British out in a white lie, or perhaps he was stupid, or perhaps he wasn't really greatly concerned about the fate of Maria Bühlen.

'A drink, then,' he suggested. 'I'm sorry I've got no vodka.'

'I thank you, but tonight I am thinking that I shall not be drinking,' Colonel Piniev said. 'If you will be excusing me, I shall return to my headquarters.'

'One for the road before you go,' Colonel Nicobar said.

'No, none for the road before I go,' Colonel Piniev said.

'Now look here, colonel,' Colonel Nicobar said. 'Of course, I know you chaps have got your orders and all that sort of thing and that you're not supposed to mix with us in case we corrupt your Marxian souls with the impurities of our bourgeois conceptions; but you ought to know as well as I do that that's all tommy faddle. How the hell are we going to plan a peace if we don't attempt to understand one another? Of course, if you've got definite orders not to drink with me personally, then I quite understand; but let me tell you this one thing: that it doesn't prevent my liking you as a man and you can tell that to your general if you like.'

'Then I am thinking I should be taking one for the road,' Colonel Piniev said. He did not smile, however, and Colonel Nicobar did not know whether he was amused or offended.

'In that case, take a chair,' Colonel Nicobar said. 'Herr Buchardt here is a soldier too. He's just been released from a Prisoner of War Camp in Russia.

He and I fought against each other on the same front in the last war and we have just been talking about our experiences. I was telling him how frightened I was in Belgium.'

'Soldiers are often frightened, but they should never show it,' Colonel Piniev said, without looking at Herr Buchardt.

'I was also going to tell him what fools soldiers were to fight for civilians,' Colonel Nicobar said. 'I think that it must be more or less the same in all countries. In England during the last war there was a silly recruiting song sung by women. One of the lines ran: "We shall love you and kiss you when you come back again," but when they came back the soldiers generally found that they had been loving and kissing somebody else.'

'It is not so in Soviet Russia,' Colonel Piniev said.

'Not quite, perhaps,' Colonel Nicobar said. 'You have a discipline which we have not got. You wouldn't stand for munition workers striking when the Army was fighting, but human nature is the same the world over, and I don't believe that the stay-at-homes are ever really grateful to those who risk their lives for them. Perhaps part of the trouble is that people can only honour a limited number of heroes: one hero, yes, two heroes, ten even, but not one hundred and seventeen and certainly not four million one hundred and seventeen.'

'It is not so in Soviet Russia,' Colonel Piniev said.

'Perhaps it is not heroes that we are requiring,' Herr Buchardt said. 'Perhaps it is cowards that we are requiring if we are really wanting to end war for ever. If every nation were having four million one hundred and seventeen soldiers who were brave enough to say, "I am too frightened to fight and therefore I shall not fight," perhaps then there would be no more wars, although I am not knowing whether it is a solution that I admire very much.'

'I do not know that I admire it either, although I quite see your point,' Colonel Nicobar said. 'If there is one thing more degrading than war it is the disgusting commercial brawl of peace, the smooth words spoken at directors' meetings, the financiers smoking big cigars and riding in limousines and the poor men wanting to smoke big cigars and ride in limousines, the foul advertisements for laxatives, lawnmowers, and life insurance, the stench of the market-place. At least soldiers are spared these things,' he went on in an effort to make Colonel Piniev and Herr Buchardt talk to each other. 'We may have to kill other men because the safe swine want to sell more sewing machines, but at least we expose ourselves to the risk of being killed in the process. It is not an absolute virtue, I know, but it is an apostolate of sorts, a dedication to a service higher than our present ambitions, a relative asceticism, if you will.'

Herr Buchardt nodded slowly, but Colonel Piniev

neither moved nor spoke, but stared sadly into the little yellow lake of his drink. Perhaps, Colonel Nicobar thought, it was impossible to expect Colonel Piniev and Herr Buchardt to talk amicably together. After all, Russia had suffered tremendously under German and Austrian occupation and now Germany and Austria were not having too good a time under Russian occupation. If Salisbury had experienced the fate of Kiev, he might not have found it so easy to talk to Oberst-Leutnant Buchardt about a soldier's life being more honourable than a civilian's. And yet there had been Coventry and the flying bombs and the rockets. He resolved to make one more effort to get the two men talking.

'Where did you fight in Russia, Herr Buchardt?' he asked.

'I was at Stalingrad,' Herr Buchardt said.

'I was at Stalingrad too,' Colonel Piniev said.

'Schlechte Schlacht,' Herr Buchardt said.

'Schlechte Schlacht,' Colonel Piniev said.

'Sometimes I think that the only way to unite the nations of the world would be for the earth to be attacked by Mars,' Colonel Nicobar said. 'We'd all love each other like hell then.'

There was a fragrance in the nuns' garden as Colonel Nicobar escorted Colonel Piniev to the gate.

'Magnolia, I think,' he said. 'The blossom will soon be out.'

200

'Magnolia blossoms are very pretty,' the Russian colonel said.

They stood for a few moments together smelling the coming spring and then each turned and went his way.

XVIII

I N SPITE OF HIS FAILURE to make Colonel Piniev and Herr Buchardt talk properly to each other, Colonel Nicobar was feeling in grand spirits next morning as he came tearing into the bathroom in his blue-and-white pyjamas and started to sing at the top of his voice:

> *For where there are wild men*
> *There must be wild women.*
> *So where did Robinson Crusoe go*
> *With Friday on a Saturday night?*

Then he remembered that he was in a convent and changed to *Onward, Christian Soldiers* instead. His content, however, did not last for long, because as soon as he arrived downstairs for breakfast, Brigadier Catlock rang up and said he wished to see him in his office immediately.

The colonel had never liked the Viennese red tramcars, which swayed irregularly across the streets of the town with two trolleys attached to each, and this morning he liked them even less than usual, because they kept swinging out of all sorts of side streets and blocking the passage of his car. 'Verfluchte Schweinhunde,' he roared at them collectively, sticking his head out of the window and managing a plural, and then he remembered the little prayer with which Reverend Mother Auxilia had said he would be able to overcome all temptation to impatience. 'Saint Walburga of Graz, charity, obedience, chastity,' he murmured, but the petition did not remove the tramcars and soothed his ire only temporarily.

'Ha,' said Brigadier Catlock as soon as Colonel Nicobar entered his office, 'there's a general turned up from the War Office on a special mission.'

'These middens are always turning up about something or other, sir,' the colonel said.

'Language, Hooky, language,' the brigadier said. 'I should have thought you'd have learned to curb that tongue of yours since you'd been living in a convent. In fact, I'd heard rumours that you'd reformed.'

'I'm always an agnostic on Tuesdays, sir,' the colonel said.

'Well, Hooky, so long as you're not a Volksdeutscher on Wednesdays, it's all right by me,' the brigadier said.

'All the same these chaps are a bit of a heartbreak, sir,' Colonel Nicobar said. 'I never seem to be able to get on with my work because I'm always having to write reports about what the writing of the reports is preventing me from doing.'

'I couldn't disagree with you less, Hooky,' the

brigadier said. 'I'm always coming up against the same thing myself. Cheer up, though. Things might have been worse: at first I thought we were going to be up against one of these little field marshal fellows, but the midden's only a full general. What these chaps get paid for beats me: buggering about all the time like blue-arsed flies in a bakery and never doing a stroke of honest work.'

The telephone on the brigadier's desk rang and he clapped the receiver to his ear. 'Catlock here. Once and for all, Gascoyne-Savoy, as far as I'm concerned cannibalization of captured enemy vehicles means cannibalization of captured enemy vehicles and if you can't understand the King's English I'm sorry for you.'

The midden came in as the brigadier banged down the receiver again and both the brigadier and the colonel rose from their seats, sprang to attention and said 'Sir!' tremendously. The midden was a kindly looking full general who wore on his breast five rows of medal ribbons all the colours of the spectrum. He sat down at the brigadier's desk which the brigadier vacated for him and began to cram his pocket handkerchief into his mouth.

'Please sit down,' the general said. 'Yes, yes, I always chew my pocket handkerchief,' he went on, observing Colonel Nicobar's astonishment. 'Pocket handkerchiefs, pencils, sheets, although I think I really prefer sheets. Worms, of course, my dear chap, worms. The R.A.M.C. have never been able to do anything about it, although they've carried out all sorts of reccies. I once chewed a towel at Shepheard's but the management was frightfully decent about it, although, of course, it was only a face towel. Ever been to Cairo? Take my advice and don't go there, especially in wartime: streets full of tight men and loose women.' He removed his handkerchief from his mouth and looked keenly at the colonel. 'You're Nicobar, aren't you?'

'Yes, sir.'

'Any relation to Nicobar in the Sixtieth?'

'First cousin, sir.'

'Really? How interesting! That fellow once stole a golf ball from me. In 1912, I think it was, at Scarborough. A Spalding Midget. Trouble about these chaps in the Sixtieth, they're shocking middens when they're subalterns and captains, but when they're forty they make damned good field officers. That right, Catlock?'

'That is correct, sir,' the brigadier said.

'The brigadier tells me that you're in charge of subversive activities,' the general went on, addressing Colonel Nicobar while Brigadier Catlock sat like a small boy with his millboard on his knee, preparing to take notes.

'The brigadier means that I am in charge of counteracting subversive activities, sir,' the colonel said.

'Same thing,' the general said. 'No use splitting hairs: wastes a lot of time.' The general went on with a little rap of authority in his voice: 'I've been sent out here to investigate a lot of things and one of them's subversive activities or as you prefer to say counteracting subversive activities. The War Office is not at all satisfied with the present position. Some of those horrible little M.P.'s with eggstains on their waistcoats have been getting up on their hindlegs in the House and asking all sorts of tomfool questions about Tito-this and Tito-that and Soviet-this and anti-Soviet that, and I believe the Warsaw Government comes into it somewhere, although I can't quite make out why. Anyway, there's nothing like getting an over-all view of the whole picture, and I've arranged for a conference to be held in Rome which you will please be kind enough to attend. The conference opens at nine hundred hours tomorrow morning. I'm a great believer in conferences, I may say. Well, Nicobar, and what's the long face about?'

'Colonel Nicobar was probably thinking that he has a lot of work to do here, sir,' Brigadier Catlock interjected.

'Well, he's going to have even more work to do in Rome,' the general said. 'I shall want a full report, Nicobar. Addressed to me personally at the War Office. Well, Catlock?'

'I was just wondering, sir, if somebody else . . .' Brigadier Catlock said.

'Nobody else, Catlock, do you hear me, nobody else,' the general said. 'But somebody else can do Nicobar's work here. What's that dim bulb Omicron doing? Sweet Fanny Adams by numbers, as usual, I suppose.'

'Colonel Omicron's in Welfare, sir,' Brigadier Catlock said. 'As a matter of fact, he's in Rome at this very moment.'

'Planning aquatic sports for next summer, no doubt,' the general said. 'Nicobar, you will fly to Rome by the plane which leaves at eleven hundred hours this morning. On your arrival in Rome you will rout out that distinguished soldier called Colonel Omicron and tell him to report back here immediately to take over your job till you return. Catlock, you will arrange the priority and kick any Red Cross hetairas off the plane that may be necessary. And if you like, Nicobar, you can borrow my car if you think it'll help you to do things quicker. No, Catlock, ho gegrapha gegrapha, an order's an order.'

With its blue leather upholstery and streamline scarlet chassis, the general's car had plenty of sex-appeal, but luckily it had speed as well, for the colonel required it if he was going to get back to the convent, pack, and arrive out at the airfield at Schwechat in time for the departure of the aeroplane.

When he arrived at the convent, he found that his

batman, as usual, had gone up to barracks on some probably frivolous errand, but Schwester Kasimira heard him come in and volunteered to help him with his packing. He was standing with his overcoat open helping her to bundle things into his suitcase when Reverend Mother Auxilia, passing along the corridor, heard their excited voices and came in to enquire what was happening.

'The Herr Oberst is going to Rome,' Schwester Kasimira explained, as she squeezed the toothpaste up from the bottom of the colonel's tube and screwed the top on properly. 'Is it not wonderful? Perhaps he will have time to see the Holy Father. Perhaps even God will give him a great grace and he will be converted, although I have been hearing that Rome is not a very good place for being converted in, which is hard to understand, since Almighty God willed that the Head of His Church should live there.'

'Is this true, Herr Oberst?' Reverend Mother Auxilia asked.

'Unfortunately, yes, Reverend Mother,' the colonel said, trying to straighten out a leg of his pyjamas which had become entangled inside the other. 'A beastly conference. General's orders. And I don't know how long I'll be away. Plane leaves Schwechat at eleven hundred hours which doesn't give a chap much time. Sometimes I wish these highly paid officers would be a little more considerate. Can't even take my batman with me. I don't suppose I'd be allowed to, anyway, but even if I were I couldn't because as usual the little shocker's nowhere to be found. Oh, I know he's got an immortal soul, Reverend Mother, but at this moment I'd appreciate the fact a little more if I had the power to call down punishment on it.'

'In that case, Herr Oberst, I shall be your batboy,' Reverend Mother Auxilia said.

'Decent of you, Reverend Mother,' the colonel said. 'I'm sure you'd do a much better job of work than that cigarette-sucking scum McCosh.'

'I mean, Herr Oberst, that I am coming with you to Rome,' Reverend Mother said.

'Eh?' the colonel said.

'I mean, Herr Oberst, that I am coming with you on that aeroplane to Rome,' Reverend Mother Auxilia said.

'Look here, Reverend Mother, that's quite impossible,' the colonel said. 'You don't understand. The authorities would never wear it.'

'I am going to see His Holiness the Pope,' Reverend Mother Auxilia said. 'In 1585 our Holy Founder flew to Rome to see Pope Sixtus the Fifth; in 1946 I am going to fly to Rome to see Pope Pius the Twelfth.'

'Look here, Reverend Mother, a joke's a joke, I know, but you don't seem to understand that I've to get a move on,' the colonel said.

'What you do not seem to be understanding, Herr Oberst, is that I am not joking,' Reverend Mother said and walked out of the room.

She didn't appear to be either, for when he got downstairs the colonel found her sitting in the back of the general's car, with a small black travelling bag on her knee.

'You see, I have not kept you waiting, Herr Oberst,' she said.

The colonel was in a quandary. He could not very well ask the driver to eject her from the car nor could he eject her himself. It was also unlikely that the nuns, who were her spiritual subordinates, would be willing to help him. And it was already half-past ten, which did not give him too much time if he were to reach the aerodrome by eleven. And Reverend Mother was a big bulky woman and she looked very much as if she were determined to go on sitting there.

'Look here, Reverend Mother, for the last time,' he said.

'I quite agree, Herr Oberst: for the last time,' Reverend Mother Auxilia said.

'Please to be taking Reverend Mother with you, Herr Oberst,' Schwester Kasimira began to plead. 'Bitte schön, Herr Oberst, bitte schön.'

'It seems that I shall have to be taking her to the aerodrome anyway, and even for that I shall probably get into trouble,' the colonel said, tossing his suitcase in beside the driver and himself getting in beside the Reverend Mother Auxilia. 'If this is your idea of spiritual whoopee, Reverend Mother, I am afraid it is not mine.'

'Gute reise, gute reise,' Schwester Kasimira said, waving her hand as the car drove off.

This time the colonel did not shout 'Verfluchte Schweinhunde!' at the tramcar-drivers, although they blocked his way several times, because he was too angry with Reverend Mother Auxilia to bother about tramcars. He sat there, huddled in his overcoat, wondering what he would do with her on his arrival at the aerodrome and whether it would be quite in order for him to send her back home again in the general's car.

'I am understanding that you are very angry with me, Herr Oberst, but perhaps you will not be so angry when I shall have explained,' Reverend Mother began as they shot across the Schwarzenbergplatz and turned up the Rennweg. 'You have been complaining since a long time that the cardinals and bishops of the Church have not spoken out the true things of the Christian religion in words that the common and sorrowing people of the earth could understand. You have said even that that was one of the reasons that you were not being a Christian. And the Russian colonel has been saying the same things and the brother of Schwester Kasimira also has been saying the same things, so that I have been forced to believe you. That is what I am going to be saying to the Pope when I am reminding His Holiness of the visit that our Holy Founder, Saint Walburga of Graz, paid to his predecessor in 1585. I am going to be asking His Holiness to be saying one clear very much all out thing which will make simple the gospel of Christ to those who are needing so badly to accept His teaching and to become good.'

'Reverend Mother, I know, I know,' the colonel said. 'I appreciate all you say, but what you're asking me to do is quite impossible.'

'Please to be reflecting a little, Herr Oberst,' Reverend Mother Auxilia went on. 'Please to be thinking of all the unhappy people in the war, please to be thinking of all the men like yourself and like Colonel Piniev and like the brother of Schwester Kasimira, who are wanting to see the light, but who are not seeing it, because the Pope and his cardinals and bishops have not been holding Christ's lamp at the right angle, so that communists and Russians and Chinese and South Americans and even Japanians and everybody else shall understand and so there shall be no more unkindness and hurt and fire and wandering families on the earth. Please to be reflecting a little, Herr Oberst.'

The colonel allowed himself to be tempted for a moment. After all, big things always came from small beginnings. Hitler and Mussolini had been small bad beginnings. Why shouldn't Reverend Mother Auxilia be a small good beginning? Why

shouldn't she, like Saint Francis and Saint Ignatius
Loyola and Saint Teresa of Avila, and perhaps like
her Holy Founder, Saint Walburga of Graz, before
her, shake up the sloth of the Universal Church,
which, when all was said and done, could provide
the only alternative to communism and the atom
bomb. Civilisation was threatened as never before
in history. Only one thing could save it: the conscious pursuit of goodness by at least a majority of
the world's inhabitants. And if the Pope were really
to put the skids under his bishops, priests, and deacons ... He pulled himself up quickly. The thing
wasn't within his terms of reference, as Brigadier
Catlock would say.

'Reverend Mother, please believe that I would do
all in my power to help you in such a mission, but
that it is strictly outside my competence to get you a
seat on that plane to Rome,' he said. 'Hang it all,
the brigadier had to arrange my own passage.'

'Herr Oberst, Almighty God will get me on the
aeroplane,' Reverend Mother Auxilia said.

There was no answer to that one, the colonel
decided, as they entered the Russian Zone and
swung out under the wooden archway onto the high-
road. As they overtook lorries packed with Russian
soldiers standing up like pencils in a box, he longed
for a discipline to come to the world, so that men
might know that the more they pursued their own
ends, the less they would attain them. The dissent-

ing manufacturers in England in the early nineteenth century had not, in the first instances at any
rate, amassed wealth because they sought it; they
had amassed wealth because their religion had
made them industrious. He was still thinking about
the dissenting manufacturers in the early nineteenth
century when the car rode through the ruins of
Schwechat to a standstill in front of the aerodrome,
where an aircraftsman was walking about with his
hat on and with a cigarette dangling from his lips.
His unsoldierlike appearance made the colonel so
angry that his eyes were poaching up to a recrimi-
natory size long before the young pilot officer approached.

'Here's your ticket, sir,' the officer said. 'Air-
craft's ready. We were just ticking over till you
came.' He motioned in the direction of an aeroplane, standing about fifty yards away.

'Who is that woozy scalawag over there?' the
colonel thundered, brandishing his stick at the untidy aircraftsman. 'Look here, young man, I know
the R.A.F.'s done a fine job of work and that we
shouldn't have won the war without you, but can't
you get that chap to understand that he's scarcely
contributing to the prestige of Empire by wandering
around looking like a scruffy organ-grinder. For
one thing, we're in an ex-enemy country, inhabited
by people who've been used to the discipline of the
German army, and for another, this is the Russian

Zone, and it's scarcely a good advertisement to the Soviets.'

'I know, sir, but my wrong doesn't make your right,' the officer said.

'What in the name of Thor and Woden do you mean?' the colonel asked.

'I mean that you've no right to bring unauthorized Austrian civilians on to the airfield,' the officer said.

'I beg your pardon,' the colonel said.

'That nun in there has no right to be here,' the officer said.

'Not only has that nun, as you so rudely term her, a perfect right to be here, but she is also flying with me to Rome,' the colonel said, letting his temper swing right out of him. 'Look here, young man, do you know who you're talking to?'

A change came over the officer's expression as he looked at the colonel's shoulderstraps.

'I beg your pardon, sir, I'm sure,' he said. 'You see, I hadn't realized and I distinctly understood Brigadier Catlock to say . . . But, of course, it's all right for the lady to go to Rome, if you say that you're willing to take the responsibility.'

'Of course I'll take the responsibility,' the colonel said.

'And of course you'll have to make things right at the other end,' the officer said.

'Of course, I'll make things right at the other end,' the colonel said.

'Herr Oberst, I was always telling you that Almighty God would be getting me on the aeroplane,' Reverend Mother Auxilia said to the colonel as he stood aside for her to climb up the steps.

Far below them stretched the academic sea, friendly, like a pale blue quilt. Colonel Nicobar and Reverend Mother Auxilia sat side by side in the Dakota, sandwiched in between two layers of Unrra. The colonel was beginning to be sorry that his outburst of temper had led him into the indiscretion of intruding Reverend Mother Auxilia into Italy. He was also beginning to be uncertain as to how he was going to be able to manage her exit from the airfield at Rome and to doubt how far his rashness would contribute to the conversion of the world.

'Ten thousand feet,' he said to Reverend Mother Auxilia so that she would not see how disturbed he was.

'Our Holy Founder, Saint Walburga of Graz, flew at twenty thousand feet and she didn't touch down at Udine,' Reverend Mother Auxilia said.

The colonel gave it up after that, thankful that it was difficult to talk in an aeroplane, although the Unrra witches behind seemed to be doing their best, yapping away through their big tusky teeth when they weren't too busy guzzling.

'Have a biccy, general,' one of the Unrra witches said, leaning over and holding out a paper bag.

'I am sorry, young woman, but I never eat biscuits,' the colonel shouted above the roar of the propeller.

'A piece of choccy, then, general?' the Unrra witch persisted.

'I am sorry, young woman, but I never eat chocolate, and what is more I am not a general,' the colonel said.

'What does he say, Mildred?' the second Unrra witch said.

'He says that he doesn't like choccy and that he's not a general,' the first Unrra witch said.

'Jawohl, General, assolutamente generale, cross my swords and hope to die,' the second Unrra witch said. 'Not like choccy? Would you, then, a leetle feesh like?'

'Salmon paste sandwiches,' the first Unrra witch explained.

'I wouldn't eat a salmon paste sandwich if I were alone with one on a desert island,' the colonel said, and then, looking down at his shoulder straps, saw the dreadful thing that had happened: he was wearing the general's overcoat, which he must, in his hurry to depart, have taken from the peg outside the brigadier's office in mistake for his own. Dismally he understood why the pilot officer at the airfield had not raised more objections when he had insisted on taking Reverend Mother Auxilia with him on the aeroplane. More dismally he knew that nobody would ever believe that he hadn't taken the general's overcoat on purpose. Brigadier Catlock wouldn't believe it. The general himself wouldn't believe it. There'd be no end of a stink. Probably there'd be a court-martial. He'd be lucky if he got off with being reduced to lieutenant-colonel again. He might even be dismissed the service. There seemed to be no limit to the number of links in the chain of possible catastrophes.

When he had become sufficiently accustomed to his dismay to be able to communicate it to another, he attempted to tell Reverend Mother Auxilia what had happened.

'Reverend Mother, I've been and gone and done it,' he said.

'Of course you have, Herr Oberst, but I am still thinking that it was a little Almighty God too,' Reverend Mother Auxilia said.

'I mean I have taken the general's overcoat by mistake,' the colonel said.

'And is that so very important?' Reverend Mother Auxilia asked. 'Surely the general will be able to wear your overcoat until you will have returned to Vienna. You must both be the same largeness of man, otherwise it would not have been possible for you to have taken his overcoat by mistake.'

'The general's not staying in Vienna,' the colonel said. 'He's one of those War Box wallahs that swan around putting their fingers in other people's pies.

218

Besides, it's not the overcoat that matters; it's the badges of rank,' he tried to explain, pointing to the crossed swords and the crown and the star on his shoulder. 'It's like a canon wearing a mitre, if you understand what I mean.'

'According to the Ambrosian rite canons are allowed to wear mitres when a bishop is pontificating,' Reverend Mother Auxilia said.

'My dear Reverend Mother, this is not the Ambrosian rite, but the British Army,' the colonel said. 'Don't you understand that I've done a terrible thing? I've laid myself open to the charge of having attempted to pass myself off as a general when I am only a colonel. That's why that silly young pipsqueak allowed me to take you on this aeroplane: because he thought I was a general.'

'Herr Oberst, are you wanting to know what I am thinking?' Reverend Mother Auxilia asked. 'I am thinking that it wasn't you that took that overcoat by mistake; it was our Holy Founder, Saint Walburga of Graz.'

'I'd like to see Brigadier Catlock wearing that one,' the colonel said. 'Or a court-martial.'

'Herr Oberst, I can see that you are not a great believer in the supernatural order,' Reverend Mother Auxilia said. 'I am repeating, therefore, that it is my opinion that it was our Holy Founder, Saint Walburga of Graz, who inspired you to take your general's overcoat. She was doing so in order that I might fly to Rome, as she has already done in 1585, in order to tell the Holy Father that he must be giving counsel to the nations of the world in a clear and understandable language. Therefore, you will be having no need to worry. Saint Walburga of Graz, who inspired you to take your general's overcoat, will also be inspiring your general to understand why you have been taking his overcoat and even to rejoice that you have taken his overcoat, for so noble and so worthy a purpose. And in any case I shall speak to the Holy Father about it, in order that he may explain to all the people of the earth about your general's overcoat at the same time as he will be explaining to them about leading a good and Christian life.'

'But, Reverend Mother ———' the colonel began.

'Please, Herr Oberst, to be allowing me to be thinking about the important message which I shall soon be delivering to the Holy Father,' Reverend Mother said.

The colonel saw that there was no real help to be obtained from Reverend Mother Auxilia. Brooding on in silence over his misery, he decided that the only thing to do was to send the general a signal explaining matters as soon as he reached Rome. In order to get Reverend Mother off the aeroplane, he would keep the general's overcoat on until they had passed the control at Ciampino, and, if necessary blast his way through as he had done in Vienna.

He would have to pretend, of course, that he hadn't noticed his mistake until he had arrived in Rome, and even then there'd be the deuce of a row, much worse than if he'd tried to infiltrate a pretty girl from Ensa, a misdemeanour which generals could more easily understand. And Reverend Mother Auxilia could get back to Vienna under her own steam or her Holy Founder Saint Walburga's steam or the Pope's steam or anybody's steam so long as it wasn't his.

'General, isn't this a ducky little cigarette lighter?' The first Unrra witch was popping her head over the back of the colonel's chair again, ogling him with gluey eyes. 'Of course, I know I mustn't light it in the plane, but I just wanted to show it to you and to tell you how well it works. A boy friend gave it to me; of course, he's not really a boy friend, because he's a chartered accountant. I think there's nothing more irritating than a lighter which won't work in a train on a long journey, don't you?'

'Young woman, I think that there are at least two things more irritating than a lighter which won't work in a train on a long journey,' the colonel said. 'One of them's being disembowelled by the Gestapo and the other's being talked at by you.'

'Oh, you rude man,' the Unrra witch said.

Spiralling down over the roofs of Rome, the colonel looked at his watch.

'Just a little over three hours,' he said to Reverend Mother Auxilia.

'In 1585, our Holy Founder, Saint Walburga of Graz, did it in under two,' Reverend Mother Auxilia said.

In the waiting room at Ciampino, the wireless was drooling out a turgid ooze of slimy terpsichorean moan, because in the modern world there had to be music all the time, the muckier the merrier. The colonel tried not to listen to the words, which were about moon and swoon and love and dove and stars above, and he hoped that Reverend Mother Auxilia wasn't listening to them either, because their significant meaninglessness would serve only to increase her conviction that her Holy Founder, Saint Walburga of Graz, was right all along the line. His ruse of saying 'two' as he had handed in his ticket and telling Reverend Mother Auxilia not to report at the security-check desk had succeeded and he hadn't had to throw the weight of his bogus rank about. He was now drafting out a signal to Brigadier Catlock. His practised hand ran swiftly over the paper:

PERSONAL FOR BRIGADIER CATLOCK FROM
    COLONEL NICOBAR   SUBJECT IS GENERAL'S
    OVERCOAT
ONE.   REGRETFULLY ASCERTAIN ON AR-
          RIVAL IN ROME THAT AM WEARING
          GENERAL'S OVERCOAT
TWO.   OVERCOAT WAS REMOVED BY ME

THIS MORNING FROM PEGS OUTSIDE YOUR OFFICE IN MISTAKE REPEAT MISTAKE FOR MY OWN WHICH WAS ALSO HANGING THERE

THREE   AM ARRANGING FOR OVERCOAT TO BE FLOWN BACK TO VIENNA IMMEDIATELY

FOUR   PLEASE EXPRESS TO GENERAL EXTREME PERSONAL REGRET FOR ANY INCONVENIENCE CAUSED TO HIM AS A RESULT OF ACTION DESCRIBED IN PARA TWO ABOVE

It took the colonel some little time to arrange the despatch of both the signal and the overcoat and by that time the bus for Rome was waiting. Reverend Mother Auxilia and the colonel both clambered in and so did the Unrra witches, who now numbered four, as the two who had been sitting behind them in the plane were now reinforced by the two who had been sitting in front. They all scowled at the colonel, who did his best not to scowl back, but looked instead at the blue, gold, and green afternoon rolling by and was glad he no longer had any overcoat, because it was already much warmer in Rome than in Vienna.

'I have made up my mind to be quite frank with the Holy Father,' Reverend Mother suddenly began. 'I shall tell him just what you and the Colonel Piniev and the brother of Schwester Kasimira have said. I shall tell him about communism having usurped the place of Christianity in appealing to the young and to the dissatisfied. I shall tell him that what men require is an honest and fearless statement of the essential charity of our religion, and that once the ordinary man shall have been convinced of our sincerity of purpose, he will no longer hesitate to submit himself to our discipline. Please, Herr Oberst, to be thinking a little of how lovely and fresh and new the world will be when it has heard the Holy Father's message and is again Christian. Please to be understanding how wars cannot come again when the peoples of the earth are knowing both the truth about our Lord and practising His teaching and knowing that they cannot really love their neighbour unless they are loving God also. Latin Christians will no longer be tired and sleepy, and will cease to lie and steal and lust and murder and be treacherous, and Nordic Christians will be having Faith to guide them, when all men shall be convinced that what Jesus Christ said was true. In India, in China, in Japan, the sanctuary lamp will burn in churches and chapels and in Moscow the Blessed Sacrament shall be carried in procession past the Kremlin.' As she turned her earnest, eager face to him, the colonel could see the tears shining behind her glasses. 'Please, Herr Oberst, to be understanding how beautiful it all will be.'

'Please believe, Reverend Mother, that I want all these things as much as you do,' the colonel said.

'Only perhaps it's not going to be as easy as you think. The children of men are fatty and degenerate in their hearts and His Holiness will have his job cut out if he is going to compel them as well as to convince them.'

'But, Herr Oberst, always have you been saying that it was the cardinals and the bishops and the priests who were being degenerate in their hearts and that all that was necessary was for the Pope to say a brave and a true thing that all perplexed men would be understanding,' Reverend Mother Auxilia said. '"Ut unum sint." Our Lord wants that, so the Holy Father must want it too.'

Reverend Mother Auxilia said that she was going to stay with the nuns of a sister house in the Via Quattro Fontane, but that she would prefer the colonel to take her straight to the Vatican, where she imagined that she would have no difficulty in arranging a private audience, in view of the urgency of her mission.

'Well, here's hoping His Holiness is going to talk turkey,' the colonel said as he left her on the steps of Saint Peter's.

'Of course he'll talk turkey,' Reverend Mother Auxilia said. 'After all, I've been knowing Eugene ever since he was an altar boy.'

As he watched Reverend Mother Auxilia waddle away up the steps of the Vatican, the colonel realised how much he was beginning to love the little round determined woman. Then he decided that he had better attempt to find Colonel Omicron, whose location in Rome he had, in his hurry, omitted to ascertain before leaving Vienna. As he was wondering where to begin his search, a full colonel with a monocle came up the steps towards him.

'Oh, hello, old boy,' the other full colonel said.

'Sorry, old boy, but I don't frightfully,' Colonel Nicobar said.

'I say, old boy, but aren't you H. de Vere Stacpoole?' the other full colonel asked.

'Sorry, old boy, but I'm not frightfully,' Colonel Nicobar said.

'I'm sorry, old boy, but I did like his book *The Green Monsoon*,' the other full colonel said.

'You mean *The Red Typhoon*,' Colonel Nicobar said.

'Something like that, old boy,' the other full colonel said. 'Anyway, it educated me.'

'I'm glad of that,' Colonel Nicobar said. 'I say, do you happen to have run across a cad called Colonel Omicron?'

'Hell of a red face and mean little boozy eyes?' the other full colonel asked.

'That's him,' Colonel Nicobar said.

'Dim bulb?' the other full colonel asked.

'Doesn't know the difference between a bee and a bull's knee,' Colonel Nicobar said.

'A bit of a dog-stealer?' the other full colonel asked.

'A thorough midden,' Colonel Nicobar said.

'Hasn't a clue?' the other full colonel asked.

'Never had a sausage,' Colonel Nicobar said.

'Small world, isn't it?' the other full colonel said. 'Old Blinker Omicron and I have been pals for years. As a matter of fact, I'm very fond of old Blinker.'

'Look here, old boy, what I want to know about old Blinker is where is he,' Colonel Nicobar said.

'Of course, old boy,' the other full colonel said. 'Well, as a matter of fact, old Blinker's down here on a conference on Welfare, but there's no conference today and he's staying at the Eden, but you won't find him there.'

'I must thank you for being so explicit,' Colonel Nicobar said. 'It is not every day that one encounters such precision.'

'Don't mention it, old boy,' the other full colonel said. 'Only too glad to oblige a friend. As a matter of fact, old Blinker's having the afternoon off. He said something about going to see Santa Maria Maggiore, as he was very fond of culture, and then about a marchesa being on the marsala and that he was going to see her, as he liked both marsala and marchesas.'

'Thanks awfully, old boy,' Colonel Nicobar said. 'Well, if you don't mind, I think I'll be toddling.'

'So sorry you're not H. de Vere Stacpoole,' the other full colonel said. 'Damned fine book *The Purple Pontoon*.'

'You mean *The Yellow Cocoon*,' Colonel Nicobar said.

'Perhaps I do,' the other full colonel said. 'If I were you I'd try Santa Maria Maggiore first.'

Colonel Nicobar took the other full colonel's advice and tried Santa Maria Maggiore first. The taxi-driver manifested his readiness to become an energetic and vigilant Latin Christian by attempting to charge the colonel thrice the legal fare, but the colonel rebuked him with an eloquent vehemence of which he was certain Saint Walburga of Graz would not have approved.

Colonel Omicron wasn't in Santa Maria Maggiore, praying or blearing at the side chapels or anything; but a great big bishop in partibus infidelium was there, strolling arrogantly across the basilica. A woman knelt to kiss his ring and the bishop extended his hand coldly with the deliberate disinterest of Brigadier Catlock acknowledging a salute from a lance-corporal. Scrofulous children in rags ran about the church begging, but the bishop passed on with no pity in his eyes. Watching him with dismay, the colonel hoped that, despite the bishop's precise belief in the unity and indivisibility of the Trinity, he would roast in hell with whores and pot boys for all eternity.

Priests came out of the sacristy in procession and slouched along to lacerate the liturgy at a side altar. Wearing the bored expressions of bandits in a brothel, they did not appear to be worrying about the peace

of Christ in the reign of Christ being the only thing
that could save the world from communism, anarchy,
and the atom bomb. The scrubby, scruffy pot-
bellied presbyters shuffled into the sanctuary and
amazingly began to say words of beauty: 'Deus, in
adjutorium meum intende; Domine ad adjuvandum
me festina.' Listening to the celestial thunder, the
colonel began to hope that they were, as Reverend
Mother Auxilia would say that they were, priests of
God all the same, old high-up windows in the world
through whose grime the grace of God could still
filter. 'O God,' the colonel prayed, plopping
briefly down on his knees, 'shake up Thy Church and
clear the stinkers and the middens out of it, and
make all things plain again.' Then, raising his eyes,
he saw that an Italian woman had prayed there
with him, in a pencilled scrawl on a pillar: 'Santa
Maria, Madre di Dio, pregate per noi, che siamo
tanto afflitte.' Cheered by this simple expression of
distress, the colonel went out again.

This time the taxi-driver tried to charge him only
twice the legal fare, so the colonel contented himself
with upbraiding him in a minor key. The marchesa,
although apparently not on the marsala, was in.
Wearing a black silk frock, she was lying on a sofa,
showing the long white autobahn of her acquiescent
thigh. She was very pleased to see the colonel,
although Colonel Omicron wasn't, because he was
there, too, with as much guilt on the crimson carpet

229

of his countenance as thirty years' bibbing and tip-
pling would permit.

'Ah, colonello, you are a knotty buoy, not having
been to see me since for so long,' the marchesa
greeted, extending a high hand from which the
fingers dripped like icicles. 'And questo Bleenker is
also a knotty buoy and that is why I am calling him
my porco colonello '

'Socrates once said that every man had the choice
of being a contented hog or a discontented philos-
opher,' Colonel Nicobar said.

'Now, look here, Hooky, don't you start getting
up-stagey just because you're living with a lot of
holy hens in Vienna,' Colonel Omicron said.

'Now, knotty buoys, no quarrelling, please,' the
marchesa said. 'Remember that we are all Allies
and ave won the war together. Ookee, I was not
altogether understanding what you were saying
about philosophers. Please tell me, because as this
porco Bleenker will tell you I am very interested in
philosophy.'

'I said that Socrates said that every man had the
choice of being a porco contento or a filosofo discon-
tento,' Colonel Nicobar said.

'I am pleased that I am not a peeg glad,' the
marchesa said. 'I think though that Bleenker is a
beeg peeg glad.'

'Now look here, Desdemona,' Colonel Omicron
protested.

'You know it is only for fun, Bleenker,' the marchesa said, patting Colonel Omicron's cheek. 'Always I am liking my funny beeg man with the very much moustache and the rather eyes sticking out. Yes, Ookee, and oo are these oly ens Bleenker says you were living with in Vienna?'

'That's Blinker's way of saying nuns,' Colonel Nicobar explained. 'I'm billeted in a convent.'

'My late usband, il caro marchese, the filthy ole coal-eaver, was very religious too,' the marchesa said.

'She means that her husband was a coal-owner,' Colonel Omicron explained.

'And that he was always religious and that sometimes he got dirty when he went down the mine,' Colonel Nicobar said.

'I am meaning nothing of the kind,' the marchesa said. 'I am meaning that the caro marchese was always dirty and that sometimes he got religious when he went down the mine. And now, Ookee, please be telling me about the peace.'

'The peace is very much on,' Colonel Nicobar said. 'In fact, it's so much on that Blinker's got to fly back to Vienna immediately.'

'Poor brave Bleenker, aving to go back to the peace,' the marchesa said.

XIX

SHE CAME TO HIM in her white frock through the trees. They stood together in the darkness at the edge of the lake, which shimmered like a mirror held in the socket of the hills. Her dress billowed in brief beauty in the breeze and then was still, and the dress shining in the lake was still, too, reflected upside down, like the chalice of a flower.

'Holding hands like nobody's business,' Twingo said.

'I am thinking that I am knowing now what that means,' Maria said.

'An English writer called Arnold Bennett once said that any ordinary man could be equally happy with any one of at least ten thousand girls and that any girl could be equally happy with any one of at least ten thousand men,' Twingo said.

'I am not thinking that I believe that,' Maria said.

'I don't believe it either,' Twingo said.

'Please to be near me again, presto subito,' she said.

'I like loving you because you are so peaceful,' he said. 'I like loving you in different dresses, but I think I could go on loving you in the same dress.'

His hands ran over her, stroking her hair, closing her eyelids so that she looked like a statue, and lifting away gently when he wanted to see her eyes again. 'Maria darling, I am so very happy when I am like this with you.' He held her face a little away from him and she suddenly seemed to him very young with her ears showing so small. 'I think that I am beginning to be no longer afraid of you, and yet, as soon as you go away from me, I shall be afraid of you again. I am afraid of you when you look too beautiful and I am afraid of you when you walk away from me without turning round, because I am afraid that God may have worked an alchemy in you and that you may no longer love me.'

'Please to be near me,' she said. 'I am liking it so very much when you are near me.'

'No longer afraid?' he asked.

'I am knowing that I am no longer needing to be afraid when I am here with you,' she said.

'When we are together in England we must not allow habit to kill our enchantment,' he said. 'Personally I am not only in favour of separate beds and separate rooms, but even of separate houses and separate streets. Napoleon was always in such a hurry that the scabbard of his sword tore the dresses of his mistresses when he went to see them. Personally I am all in favour of the procedure. There is nothing that can kill delight as quickly as a pair of braces seen through an open bathroom door.'

They both giggled at the joke and he kissed her while she was still laughing. Then she came upon him, the full breathing of her, and laid the trouble of her body against his. The rain of her hair fell over his cheek and he knew in joy the gust of her lips and the balm of her breasts and the night went on in darkness above the lake.

XX

WHO IS THAT MIDDEN?' Colonel Omicron
asked as he bounced into the office and found the
Rumanian general searching with Audrey for loyal
Rumanians, who had fought for the four freedoms
and who now numbered only *six hundred*, so the general said, because the others had been found in Spain
and southern Ireland.

'Please tell this vairy nobel courteous gentleman
that I am not come here to dally-dilly, but to help the
progress of democracy,' the Rumanian general said,
looking hurt under the cartwheel of his big hat.

'That's true, Blinker,' Audrey said. 'General
Koposchin is extremely progressive.'

'C'est vrai, mon colonel,' the Rumanian general
said.

'Je suis partisan de tout foutre en l'air: l'église, la
bourse et la bourgeoisie.'

'So you see, Blinker, he's one of us,' Audrey said.
'All out for law and order.'

'Miss Quail, I would remind you that we are on
parade,' Colonel Omicron said, with an attempt at
sternness.

'I beg your pardon, sir,' Audrey said.

'Je suis à la recherche de six cents roumains qui ont tout sacrifié pour la cause alliée,' the Rumanian general went on.

'Surely that's the business of Displaced Persons Division at Allied Commission Headquarters,' Colonel Omicron said. 'Say sah, mong jaynayral, ally voir lay Dee Pees à Schönbrunn et Robert sayra votre oncle.' He waved a gesture of dismissal to the Rumanian general and entered Colonel Nicobar's office whither he beckoned Audrey to follow him.

'Yes, sir,' said Audrey, smiling at him through a pout of mismanaged maquillage.

'The subject is subversive activities, Miss Quail,' Colonel Omicron said, seating himself pompously at Colonel Nicobar's desk. 'I've been asked, as perhaps you know already, to take over until Colonel Nicobar comes back from Rome, and I should be very grateful if you would tell me the form.'

'The form, sir, is that we're out to stamp out all seditious propaganda uttered by anti-Tito Slovenes, anti-Tito Croats, pre-1939 Russian émigrés, anti-Soviet Russians, anti-Warsaw Poles, anti-Budapest Hungarians, and to aid in the detection and apprehension of all war criminals,' Audrey said.

'Sounds simple enough to me,' Colonel Omicron said. 'I never did like these beastly reds, anyway.'

'But these people are whites, sir, and some of them are blacks,' Audrey said. 'You see, sir, it's all terribly political.'

'Continue, please,' Colonel Omicron said.

'You see, sir, politics have changed since before the war,' Audrey explained. 'Before the war the reds were seditious and the blacks and the whites were loyal, but now the reds have won the war and so they're loyal and the blacks and the whites are seditious, and now we've got to stamp out their political opinions, although we've still got to respect them, too, because that's democracy.'

'I see, Miss Quail, yes, yes, I think I am beginning to see,' Colonel Omicron said. 'And Nazis? Where do they come into the picture?'

'They were browns before the war, but I suppose that one would have called them whites,' Audrey said.

'But I thought you said just now that the whites were loyal before the war,' Colonel Omicron said.

'That's where the real complication begins, sir,' Audrey said. 'You see, geography comes into it as well as politics. A white who lived outside Germany or Italy before the war was loyal, but a white who lived inside Germany or Italy was seditious, and a black who lived inside Germany was loyal, because he was up against the reds, but of course they're both seditious and subversive now because the reds have won, although in England it's both seditious and subversive to be red because that's where the pinks come in.'

'And Volksdeutsche?' Colonel Omicron asked. 'I seem to remember reading about them somewhere.'

'They were mostly black before the war until Hitler overran them and made them white, and of course they're white still, because the reds don't think they're really red and are frightened they'll turn black again,' Audrey said.

'I must thank you, Miss Quail, for having explained the set-up so clearly,' Colonel Omicron said. 'There's just one other thing I want to ask you. I didn't see Major McPhimister as I passed through your office just now. Where is he?'

'He's in the Zone, sir,' Audrey said.

'On duty, I suppose?' Colonel Omicron said.

'I'm afraid not, sir.' The tears came to Audrey's eyes as she thought of Twingo loving Maria when he wouldn't love her. 'Please don't ask me more, sir,' she said, gulping down her sorrow.

'Miss Quail, I am afraid I must insist on knowing,' Colonel Omicron said. 'Please remember that for the moment I am both your and Major McPhimister's commanding officer. Has Major McPhimister official permission to be absent from Vienna?'

'Colonel Nicobar's permission, sir; at least, I think so, sir,' Audrey said, licking up with her long tongue at the tears which were now flowing down towards her mouth.

'What do you mean, "you think so"? Either you know or you don't know.' Colonel Omicron laid a clumsy hand on her shoulder, convinced that he knew when to be tender. 'Audrey, please.'

The gesture of sympathy and the sudden use of her Christian name were too much for Audrey. Snuffling with self-pity, she broke down completely.

'I know I've been a pig to you at times, Blinker, and I'm sorry because I know you're kind, but you see it's him I love and I've had it because he loves her,' she said.

'Audrey darling, tell me and I'll try to understand,' Colonel Omicron said.

'Sometimes I try not to hate her and to tell myself that it's not her fault that Twingo is in love with her, but usually I can't help hating her all the same,' Audrey blubbered on. 'What makes it all the more difficult is that at one time I thought she'd gone back to Russia for good and that sooner or later Twingo would fall in love with me, because a girl can generally make a man fall in love with her if she wants him to very much. Of course, I tried not to be glad when Colonel Nicobar sent her back to Russia in the first instance, although during the war she danced for the Nazis in Vienna; and I tried to be glad when she escaped and came back to the convent again and Colonel Nicobar didn't send her back because he said the Russians weren't entitled to have Volksdeutsche after all, even if they were Russian Volksdeutsche, but of course I wasn't glad, because I was loving Twingo and wanting him all for myself. And then, when Twingo persuaded Colonel Nicobar to send her down to the Zone so that the Russians wouldn't come snooping round after her any more, well, honestly, Blinker, it was too much for me, and I've cried myself to sleep every night since, because now I know definitely that I've lost Twingo for ever. That's where he is now, mooning with her in Millstatt and telling her that her eyes are like forest pools, and please believe me that I'm not being catty when I say that her eyes are not nearly as like forest pools as mine. Oh, Blinker, why is life such a nonsense at times?'

But Colonel Omicron was no longer kindly and warm and sympathetic; concentrated like an ostrich about to lay an egg, he was poising his pencil above a writing pad.

'Millstatt, did you say?' he asked.

'Yes, Blinker, but surely you're not going to . . . Please, Blinker. I wouldn't have told you if I'd thought . . .'

'Audrey, what you have just told me amounts to a breach of an international agreement on the part of Colonel Nicobar and Major McPhimister,' Colonel Omicron said. 'And what did you say this young person's name was?'

'I didn't say it was anything, Blinker, but it's Maria Bühlen, and in any case she's a Russian Volksdeutscher and doesn't require to go back,' Audrey said.

'You've just told me that Hitler made them white and that they're still white and that people who are

still white are seditious and subversive,' Colonel
Omicron said. 'Field Marshal Lord Allenby said
that the great thing about me was that, although it
took a long time to get an idea into my head, once it
got there it stayed there.' He reached for the telephone. 'Give me the Russians,' he said.

XXI

Colonel Nicobar's mission in Rome turned out to be supererogatory and when he returned to Vienna he found a note on his desk ordering him to report to Brigadier Catlock immediately. The brigadier came to the point at once.

'The general took a very dim view,' he said. 'Of course he borrowed your overcoat in return, but he was late for an appointment with another V.I.P. through having to have the badges of rank changed at the officers' shop.'

The telephone rang and the brigadier began to bellow down the mouthpiece. 'Catlock here. Of course, I'm fly-conscious. We're all fly-conscious. Everybody's fly-conscious. Look here, Gascoyne-Savoy, that's not G.H.Q. at all. That's old Tiddler Tamar. I've far too much high-level stuff to do to have time to run round pantries flicking flies off fish-cakes.'

He replaced the receiver. 'Gideon ought to have answered that one, but as usual he isn't here,' he said. 'Oh, I forgot. I was in the middle of administering a raspberry, wasn't I?'

'Such was my interpretation of our interview, sir,' Colonel Nicobar said.

'Now look here, Hooky, I don't want to be unpleasant and if it was only a matter of your having taken the general's overcoat by mistake it would be easy enough to wash the whole matter out,' the brigadier said. 'But unfortunately it isn't. I have here a report from the R.A.F. alleging that you intruded a nun into Italy and passed yourself off as a general in order to do so. Is that true, Hooky?'

'It is and it isn't, sir,' Colonel Nicobar said. 'I admit that I illegally infiltrated a nun into Italy, but the business of the general's overcoat was a genuine mistake. I only discovered the fact after the plane had taken off. That, sir, I must ask you to believe.'

'Of course I believe it, Hooky,' the brigadier said. 'I've been long enough in the army to be very good at believing. But a nun, Hooky, really! And who is the old bag, anyway?'

'She is the Reverend Mother Auxilia, superior of the convent in which you yourself billeted me, sir, and she isn't an old bag,' Colonel Nicobar said vehemently. 'She is a very holy, wise, and perspicacious woman, and I personally have a great respect and affection for her.'

'All right, Hooky: don't lose your wool,' the brigadier said. 'But even if she is all these things, what did you want to take her to Rome for?'

'I took her to Rome in order that she could have a private audience with the Pope,' Colonel Nicobar explained. 'Reverend Mother Auxilia was very distressed when I told her that the reason why a great number of men of intelligence and good faith would not accept official Christianity was because its representatives never dared to say the plain, true, fearless thing that all men could understand. When a Russian officer and an ex-Austrian officer told her the same thing as I did, Reverend Mother Auxilia began to think that there was something in it. And so she asked me to take her with me to Rome because she thought that she might be able to persuade the Pope to say the plain, true, fearless thing.'

'And so you gave in and took her,' the brigadier said. 'My God, Hooky, we'll have you a missionary next, rushing about the jungle and crying "Coo-ee, Dr. Livingstone." Go on, Hooky, I'm listening.' He smoothed the lock of white hair which gave him distinction and looked attentive.

'I didn't accede to her request at once, sir, and in the end it was only through force of circumstance, but now I am not sorry that I did so,' the colonel said. 'After all, the world is in a pretty hellish mess and the chaps in authority don't seem to be helping us out much, do they? I mean that the politicians and those who sit deliberating at high tables don't seem to be helping us out much, do they? I mean that the politicians and those who sit deliberating at high tables don't seem to have a clue and are still going on perpetrating the old error of taking the short view instead of the long view. They are prudent today in order that they themselves may be safe today instead of being good today in order that other people may be safe tomorrow. And I agree with Reverend Mother Auxilia that it is only by being good in a big way that the inhabitants of this earth may be saved from destruction. And that is why I am glad that I broke regulations and took her to Rome. After all, sir, during the war we sacrificed night after night bombers that cost fifty thousand pounds and the lives of men in order that problematical destruction might be caused to the enemy. Surely the cost of an aeroplane passage and the career of an officer is not too much to hazard in order that the nations of the world may be given one more chance of learning to live with one another?'

'Look here, Hooky, I've always been broadminded about religion, provided of course a chap isn't a Catholic or a Jew or a Baptist,' the brigadier said. 'But what you don't seem to realize is that this escapade of yours is likely to get both of us into hot water with the big noises at Allied Commission for Austria Headquarters and Vienna Inter-Allied Command.'

'I'm sorry about that, sir, but I still think that I acted for the best,' Colonel Nicobar said.

'There's one other thing,' the brigadier said. 'Whereabouts is this nun now?'

'She's still in Italy,' the colonel said. 'Before I left her in Rome, I explained that I had done all I

245

could for her and that I couldn't possibly work her passage back again. I told her that she must get back to Vienna under her own steam or that she must ask the Pope to help her. She said that she quite understood and that if the worse came to the worst she could always go on staying with some other nuns in Rome, and that one of the other nuns here could run the convent till she got back again.'

'Then she must be extruded out again immediately,' the brigadier said. 'She cannot be allowed to go on staying in Rome, exercising what you of all people ought to know are subversive activities. Just imagine for a moment what might happen to the world if she succeeded in getting the Pope to make some great galumping statement which would make the Russians religious. Stalin would never forgive us. And Tito would probably seize Trieste right away.'

'I don't think that there is much chance of her succeeding, sir, although I still think that it would be a very excellent thing indeed if she were to succeed,' Colonel Nicobar said.

'I disagree entirely,' Brigadier Catlock said. 'The whole thing's subversive and stinks to high heaven. Besides, it's against geology. I shall ring up the Travel and Frontier Control people at Headquarters and ask them to get this nun back to Vienna immediately. What did you say her name was again and where is she hanging out in Rome?'

Colonel Nicobar told the brigadier.

'Now look here, Hooky, boys will be boys, I know, but this sort of thing has got to stop,' the brigadier said. 'I ought, of course, to furnish a full report to the Allied Commission and Vienna Area and the War Office and everybody, but I am not going to do so for two reasons. First, I am not going to do so because the general himself is now safely back in London and has no knowledge of the purposes to which you are alleged to have put his borrowed top-coat. Secondly, I am not going to take any action in the matter because I am prepared to believe your statement that you yourself were unaware of the fact that you were wearing the general's overcoat when you told that pilot officer fellow that you were per-fectly willing to take full responsibility for flying the nun to Rome. But even if it was only as a full colonel that you were willing to take that responsibility, your contravention of travel control regulations still constitutes a very serious offence, and that, Hooky, as your superior officer, I am bound to point out to you. I must also add the warning that any further blob on your part will force me to reconsider my decision and to refer the whole matter to the War Office. I'm sorry to have to speak to you like this, Hooky, but that's the way things are.'

'I quite understand, sir,' Colonel Nicobar said. 'Thank you very much, sir.'

The telephone rang and the brigadier said into the

mouthpiece: 'No, Gascoyne-Savoy, I know nothing about Gresham's Law, but my wife would like to borrow a lawnmower.' He put the receiver down again.

Because he was not a severe or an unkind man at heart, but only an irritated soldier who had to earn his living by carrying out the orders of other irritated soldiers, the brigadier smiled at Colonel Nicobar.

'Good old Hooky,' he said.

XXII

THE AMERICANS WERE ENTERTAINING, and the quadripartite conviviality was going strong, too strong for Brigadier Catlock, who wanted to have a word with his Russian opposite member about Greek drachmae. The brigadier's official advisers, two lieutenant-colonels, sat beside him, but they did not detract from his impatience, because they were not speaking to each other, as each held diverging views on the inflationary aspect of documentary credits.

'How you feeling, Sadie?' an American colonel asked the pretty W.A.A.C. beside him.

'I reckon I'm feeling fine and dandy, Spike,' the pretty W.A.A.C. said. 'Why, say, I never felt happier in all my life.'

'How'm I doing, Sadie?' the American colonel asked.

'Why, you're doing fine, Spike,' the pretty W.A.A.C. said, and then turned her large liquid Turkish-delight eyes full on the brigadier. 'What you say, general? Spike's doing fine, isn't he?'

'I think that Colonel Mäusebeisser is doing very well indeed,' Brigadier Catlock said.

'Say, Spike, that's swell,' the pretty W.A.A.C.

249

said. 'The general thinks you're doing fine, too. Don't you think, general, that in Vienna they have the loveliest moon in all the world?'

This was too much for Brigadier Catlock, who didn't like being called 'general' or talking about moons. With a curt nod he got up and left the two lieutenant-colonels to talk to Sadie and himself went in search of the Russian colonel, with whom he was exceedingly anxious to speak.

'Well, of all the heels,' Sadie said.

'Well, I'll be right go to hell,' Colonel Mäusebeisser said. 'Take it from me, Sadie, that guy's a Hun. The British Army's full of Huns.'

But before he could reach the Russian colonel, Brigadier Catlock found himself confronted by the French colonel, who said that he was very anxious to talk to him.

'Mon général, j'ai toujours voulu vous exprimer ma profonde admiration pour la grande nation anglaise,' the French colonel said.

'Wee, wee,' Brigadier Catlock said.

'Car malgré tous les malentendus, des fois graves, j'en conviens, qui ont séparé nos deux peuples au cours de l'histoire, je suis le premier à constater que le peuple anglais a toujours fait preuve d'un courage magnifique,' the French colonel said.

'Wee, wee, wee,' Brigadier Catlock said.

'Et en mil neuf cent quarante quand tout semblait si sombre . . .' the French colonel said.

250

'Wee, wee, wee, wee,' Brigadier Catlock said. 'Exkewsay moi in a hurry wee, wee, wee, wee.'

'Horosho,' the Russian colonel said. 'Es smeckt Ihnen gut?'

Brigadier Catlock didn't want to have to talk to the Russian colonel about food because he wanted to get down to brass tacks right away, and he didn't want to talk about food in German because he couldn't talk German, at least not very well. He knew, however, that it would be more diplomatic to start the ball rolling by speaking about something about which the representatives of Great Britain and Soviet Russia were likely to be able to agree. He decided, therefore, to approach the subject of Greek drachmae via the uncontroversial topic of sausage rolls.

'Heisser Hund sehr gut,' he said.

'Oat doag wunderbar,' the Russian colonel said.

'Aber Greek drachmae nicht so wunderbar,' Brigadier Catlock said.

'The Union of Soviet Socialist Republics not willing to discuss Greek drachmae, only oat doag,' the Russian colonel said.

'Now look here, colonel, the matter is important; it can't be put off forever,' Brigadier Catlock said.

'The Union of Soviet Socialist Republics think that the question of the repatriation to Soviet Russia of Russian Volksdeutsche also very important,' the Russian colonel said. 'Not a little time ago we ask

251

for repatriation of Maria Bühlen hiding convent Vienna. Your Colonel Nicobar big man with red hair and one arm also living convent. Maria Bühlen handed over to us and sent back to Russia. Maria Bühlen escape, perhaps because very pretty girl, and make love to the guards, but anyway she escape and come back to Vienna. Colonel Piniev go convent and ask if there and Colonel Nicobar say no. But when Colonel Nicobar is in Rome with nun planning with the Pope an attack on the Union of Soviet Socialist Republics Colonel Omicron ring up Colonel Piniev and say Maria Bühlen all the time in the British Zone of Austria. Russia is not afraid of the Swiss Guard Divisions from the Vaticano, but Russia wants Maria Bühlen back from the British Zone of Austria. And that is why the Union of Soviet Socialist Republics not willing discuss Greek drachmae but only oat doag.'

XXIII

THIS TIME the brigadier came to the point even more immediately.

'Nicobar, the subject is Maria Bühlen,' he said. 'Last night I was informed by one of my Russian colleagues that she was in the British Zone of Austria. Who sent her there?'

'I sent her there, sir,' Colonel Nicobar said.

'And may I ask why?' the brigadier asked.

'In order that the Russians shouldn't forcibly repatriate her, sir,' Colonel Nicobar said. 'When I first handed her over to the Russians on your instructions, sir, you distinctly said . . .'

'Now look here, Hooky, we'll never get anywhere if you're going to expect me to remember every bloody silly thing I ever distinctly said,' the brigadier said.

'. . . you distinctly said, sir, that I need not hand her over, as you had had the ruling from the Displaced Persons Division that Russian Volksdeutsche were not forcibly repatriable,' Colonel Nicobar continued. 'First, sir, I informed you that Maria Bühlen had returned to Vienna in that train of expelled Jugoslav Volksdeutsche which you ordered

253

me to inspect early on Christmas morning. You told me to stick her on the wall.'

'That certainly sounds a bit more like me,' the brigadier said.

'Your final instructions, however, sir, were that I should put the matter in writing,' Colonel Nicobar said.

'Now look here, Hooky, if you expect me to read every piece of bumph that finds its way into my in-tray,' the brigadier said.

'My orders, sir, were to put the matter in writing and I did so,' Colonel Nicobar said. 'When I received no reply to my report, I concluded that I was at liberty to use my own judgment. As I knew that the Russians were theoretically entitled to repatriate her as long as she remained in Vienna and as I was under the impression that you no longer wished her to be sent back to Russia against her wishes, I sent her down to the British Zone of Austria.'

'That you had no business to do,' the brigadier said. 'And I think that you know that as well as I do.'

'According to the letter of the law, no, sir, but according to the spirit, yes,' Colonel Nicobar said.

'All I know is that your action has considerably embarrassed me in my relations with the Russians,' Brigadier Catlock said. 'And that dim bulb Omicron's ringing up Colonel Piniev and letting the cat out of the bag didn't do any good either. The silly midden ought to have come to me first. But there's no use crying over spilt milk when there's a cat around to lick it up. And you are going to be the cat: Hooky, you've got to get that girl back from the British Zone immediately and hand her over to the Russians.'

'But, sir,' Colonel Nicobar said.

'There are no "buts," Hooky,' the brigadier said.

'But Volksdeutsche aren't subversive, sir,' the colonel said.

'All Volksdeutsche are subversive if I say so, Hooky,' the brigadier said.

'But, sir,' the colonel said.

'It's an order, Hooky,' the brigadier said.

'Then, sir, it is an order which I must refuse to obey,' Colonel Nicobar said.

'I'm warning you, Hooky,' the brigadier said.

'And I'm pleading with you, sir,' Colonel Nicobar said. 'This girl has done no wrong except to escape from Russia when her parents were sent to Siberia and to disagree with the political régime at present in force in her country. One of our reasons for fighting this war was to liberate the people of Europe from tyranny, by whatever name it called itself. And one of our proudest boasts ought to be that in our Displaced Persons Camps we are maintaining at this very moment thousands of unhappy human beings who are unwilling to go home because they are afraid of the new tyranny which has been established there. Maria Bühlen is one of these thousands, sir; her case is no different from theirs.'

'Her case is different from theirs in that she is a Displaced Russian Volksdeutscher who was originally uncovered in the Innerestadt of Vienna and must consequently be considered as a Soviet citizen subject to Russian regulations,' Brigadier Catlock said. 'Once and for all, Hooky, are you or are you not going to hand this girl over?'

'I am sorry, sir, but my answer must be that I am not going to hand her over,' Colonel Nicobar said.

'In that case, Nicobar, you leave me no option,' Brigadier Catlock said. 'You are to hand over your functions once more to Colonel Omicron, who will also be given the responsibility of carrying out my order which you have just refused to obey. Pending the result of my submission of the whole matter to the War Office, you are to consider yourself temporarily unemployed. As this is the second grave breach of discipline which you have committed within a short period, I shall, of course, be forced to include the matter of your breach of travel control regulations in my report. That, I think, will be all for the moment. *Good*-morning, Nicobar.'

XXIV

WHEN MARIA BÜHLEN was brought back from Millstatt she shot herself through the breast before she could be handed over to the Russians and now she lay dying in her old room in the convent. Schwester Kasimira had explained to her how gravely she had sinned in seeking to take her own life, because it was the duty of Christians to leave it to Almighty God to send death how and when He would, and the old priest whose collar always stuck up too much at the back had been sent for, to shrive her, to anoint her, and to give her Holy Communion.

The priest was gone now and Maria lay with her eyes closed and with her hair brushed out in golden strands upon the pillow. A crucifix stood on her bedside table between two candles which Schwester Kasimira had lighted for when the priest should bring the Blessed Sacrament. The nun had, however, forgotten to remove the lotions and the ointments and the pigments from the dressing-table, and the two tiny tongues of flame burned again in tinier tongues in the silver tops of bottles and backs of mirrors, hallowing the pathetic little armoury of enticement. Twingo sat beside her, the tears streaming from his eyes.

'Macht nichts, Twingo, nicht weinen, you must not weep.' She kept her eyes closed and prayed a little, as Schwester Kasimira said she must pray, if she wanted God to forgive her: 'In Deine Hände, Herr, befehl ich meinen Geist.' Then she opened her eyes and tried to smile across her pain. 'Please to be near me as you were by the lake,' she said. 'I am liking it so very much when you are near me as you were by the lake.'

'Maria,' Twingo gulped.

'Please not to be weeping,' she said. 'Please just to be holding my hand like nobody's business.' She closed her eyes again, clasping his hand happily in hers. 'Heiligstes Herz Jesu, ich vertraue auf Dich: ich glaube auf Deine Liebe zu mir. Please, Twingo, to be thinking of me sometimes when you are being happy again with one of ten thousand other girls. Please, Twingo, not to be thinking that I am jealous, but please not to be loving her as you loved me.'

'Maria, Maria darling, you mustn't,' Twingo said.

'But I must be saying these things now because Schwester Kasimira is telling me that I shall be seeing Jesus Christ presto subito, and I shall not be seeing you again until you also shall be coming to see Jesus Christ, and then perhaps we shall not be wanting to say these things, because we shall be too holy.' She lay for a little without speaking. 'I am trying to feel glad about seeing Jesus Christ presto subito, but I am thinking that I should like to be

258

seeing you again here on earth a little bit more first,' she said and then prayed again: 'Herr, bleib bei mir, sei meine wahre Freude.'

Schwester Kasimira came in again with an open book in her hands. In her big pleated skirt she knelt down by the bed and began to read aloud from her book: 'Keiner lebt sich selber und keiner stirbt sich selber. Leben wir, so leben wir dem Herrn; sterben wir, so sterben wir dem Herrn. Darum im Leben und im Sterben sind wir des Herrn.'

So this is what life is really about, Twingo thought as he listened, living and dying unto God. He had seen men die on the battlefield, torn apart in a burst of entrails, and God hadn't seemed to have much to do with it, but Schwester Kasimira, reading away holy German words out of her big book, seemed to know that even those untidy deaths had been died unto God. As Schwester Kasimira read on, with her plain splodgy face meaning every word and Maria lay there with her eyes closed saying nothing, Twingo knelt down beside the bed, too, and tried to think about life being about living and dying unto God. Before he had met Maria, life hadn't been about God at all, but only about sherry and stocks and shares and the marchesa's silk stockings. Even after he had met Maria, life hadn't been much about God, but only about Maria herself and kissing her under the brim of her wide white hat; but now that she lay there dying because she hadn't wanted to go back to Russia, the world was all about God and he didn't think Schwester Kasimira and the nuns silly any longer.

'Süsses Herz Maria, sei meine Rettung,' Schwester Kasimira began to pray.

The dying girl opened her eyes.

'Süsses Herz Maria,' she tried to pray back and her hand stirred in Twingo's. 'Like nobody's business,' she said, and then she died.

XXV

As usual, Brigadier Catlock was talking on the telephone when Colonel Nicobar called to see him in his office for the last time. 'No, I don't know him from a bar of soap, but you can take it from me that the green fly's the thing in Cashmir, old boy,' he was saying. As soon, however, as he recognized the identity of his visitor, the brigadier laid down the receiver and addressed the colonel in a tone of genuine distress.

'Hooky, old boy, I can't tell you how sorry I am that this terrible thing has happened,' he said.

'I'm sorry too, sir,' Colonel Nicobar said. 'And poor Twingo's even sorrier. They were in love, you see, and wanted to get married.'

'I'm sorry about that, too, Hooky,' the brigadier said. He was silent for a little so that the colonel might understand that he really meant what he said. 'I still maintain, however, that I acted according to the book: although Russian Volksdeutsche are not compulsorily repatriable the girl was originally uncovered in the Innerestadt . . .'

'If you don't mind, sir, let's please not go into all that again,' the colonel said. 'What has been done

261

has been done and nothing can undo it. Without wishing in any way, however, either to be or to appear insubordinate, I shall always think that Maria Bühlen's case was one in which clemency might have been exercised. All over the world, sir, Rachel is still weeping for her children and, what is even worse, many children have no Rachel to weep for them. And unless we understand that pity is a virtue there is no hope for us.'

'That's all right, Hooky; I know just how you feel,' the brigadier said. 'There's just one other thing: about my report to the War Office . . .'

'Yes, sir?'

'I'm sorry to have to tell you that I'm afraid they're taking a poor view,' the brigadier went on. 'In fact, they go so far as to say that they refuse to discuss the matter by correspondence. Look here, Hooky, to cut the cackle, the long and the short of it is that they've issued instructions for you to relinquish your appointment here and to report back to Whitehall immediately.'

'That's quite all right by me, sir,' Colonel Nicobar said.

'Honestly, Hooky, I can't tell you how sorry I am that all this has happened,' the brigadier said.

'That's all right, sir,' the colonel said.

'You must admit, though, that you rather forced my hand,' the brigadier said.

'I admit that, sir,' the colonel said.

'All the same, Hooky, it's decent of you to take things this way,' the brigadier said.

'We're not civilians,' the colonel said.

There did not seem to be anything more to be said.

'Well, good-bye, Hooky, and all the best,' the brigadier said.

'And to you, sir,' Colonel Nicobar said.

Although it was late that evening when the colonel returned to his office, the little Austrian girl was still playing beneath the trees, because it was longer light now. With her skirt flying, she came running towards him and gave him her hand.

'Guten Abend, Mickey Mouse,' the colonel said.

'Mickey Mouse, ha, ha,' the little girl said.

'Wie Alt bist du?' the colonel asked.

'Ich bin fünf Jahre alt,' the little girl said.

This time, however, he did not ask her why she was not at school, but bent and kissed her, because he wanted to carry away with him a little of the benediction of her childhood.

XXVI

'EUGENE didn't talk turkey after all,' Reverend Mother Auxilia said to Colonel Nicobar as she sat with him at the back of the Votifkirche, where she had asked him to pray with her before he left Vienna for good. The colonel hadn't found it easy to pray, perhaps because he hadn't tried for so long, perhaps because the draught blowing through the shattered window-panes was making his non-existent fingers ache. Indeed, so sharp had been the stabs of agony that he had to get up and walk round the church in an attempt to still them. 'DEN TOTEN KAMERADEN DES WELTKRIEGES 1914–1918; FÜR HEIMAT UND VOLK' he had read engraved in gold above a list of names on a black marble plaque, and he had concluded that it wasn't only in England that humble tragedy failed to be eloquent. He was still thinking about this when he came back to wait for Reverend Mother Auxilia to finish praying.

'He didn't talk turkey, but he talked good sense,' Reverend Mother Auxilia said.

A concatenation of nonsense dimly remembered from 1920 raced irresistibly through the colonel's mind:

Oh, oh, oh, my sweet Hortense,
She ain't got money, but she's got good sense.
She's got wonderful teeth in her mouth:
One points north and the other points south.

He stifled the rigmarole against the image of a knobbly-faced priest in a shiny cassock walking down the church to pray in front of the sanctuary rails. From his ugliness and poverty it was obvious that he was a very holy priest.

'That was just what I was afraid of, Reverend Mother,' he said.

'You and I have both been wrong, Herr Oberst,' Reverend Mother Auxilia went on. 'The Pope pointed that out to me quite clearly. He was very kind, and he remembered us meeting as children, and he knew all about Saint Walburga of Graz, but he didn't think that it was due to her inspiration that you were wearing your general's overcoat.'

'I'm afraid the general doesn't think so either,' Colonel Nicobar said.

'Please to be listening to me patiently, Herr Oberst, and I shall try to be telling you what the Holy Father was saying,' Reverend Mother Auxilia said. 'I am knowing that I have caused you a lot of trouble with your superior officers and for that I am very sorry, especially as the Pope is not wishing to do the thing that you and I were wishing him to do: to speak to the nations of the world in a plain and penetrating voice. He will continue to speak,

of course, as and when the Holy Ghost moves him
and will continue to issue encyclicals.'

'Encyclicals!' the colonel said impatiently. 'But
nobody ever pays any attention to them, apart from
a lot of half-baked priests and nuns.'

'That was what the Pope was saying, although he
was perhaps not expressing himself quite that way,'
Reverend Mother Auxilia said. 'For who, Herr
Oberst, listens to Jesus Christ either, apart from a
lot of half-fried priests and monks? And Jesus
Christ has spoken very long ago, and in simple words
of meaning that could not possibly be misunderstood,
unless, Herr Oberst, they were wilfully misunderstood. The words have gone out to the ends of the
earth, Herr Oberst, ringing like bells across mountains and snows and rivers, telling man that whatso-
ever he would that men should do to him, that he
should do to them, and calling upon him to love the
Lord his God with his whole heart and with his whole
mind, and his neighbour as himself. And in order
that there should be no excuse for men not understanding, God has been allowing this lesson of love
to be expressed also by the prophets of the less true
religions of India and Japan and China, showing
men how they might be saved from themselves not
only in the next world, but in this.

'The Church, Herr Oberst, is not here to invent a
new truth, because there is no such thing as a new
truth, because truth is from all time and does not

change, because men through meddling with God's secrets have unleashed a power with which they may destroy themselves. Atomic power is not a new truth because it has been a truth or a plank in God's creation from the beginning of time: it is only an old truth recently revealed by man, but not by God. Sanctifying grace, Herr Oberst, is not a new truth either because it also has been a truth or a plank in God's creation since the beginning of time; it is only an old truth a long time ago revealed by God because it is necessary for man's salvation. And the purpose of the Church, Herr Oberst, the function of prelates, is to be guarding these old truths a long time ago revealed by God, so that they may still be the same truths to point the way to men in their trouble.'

The priest kneeling at the sanctuary rails rose and walked away into the sacristy in his shiny cassock. The wind came in through the jagged edges of the windows in the apse and flapped the white cloth on the altar and blew the candle flames squint. The colonel's ghostly fingers began to ache again, but he did not notice the pain much because he was too busy thinking about what Reverend Mother Auxilia had just said.

'I am believing that you are not understanding altogether what I have been saying,' Reverend Mother Auxilia said. 'You are perhaps wondering why old truths should be requiring a Church and a hierarchy to keep them the same truths as when they were first revealed to man by God. Well, I shall tell you: even truths revealed by God can be foolishly reported by the crowd and even distorted by evil men for their own purposes. Let me give you an example: both Hitler and Mussolini knew in their own hearts that it was their duty to love their fellow-men, but instead they denied God's teaching and proclaimed that might was right and that force was virtue.

'If there had been no Church down the ages to conserve God's truths, if there had been no priests and deacons to repeat God's message and to explain it, you and I would perhaps not be knowing that it was our duty to succour our friends and our enemies in their distress. And to whom else would you entrust God's counsel today? To the White House? To Downing Street? To the Elysée? To the Kremlin? No, Herr Oberst, churchmen have often been weak and vain and ambitious and cowardly, but never has the Church of God allowed the lamp of God quite to go out, and never has the Church been teaching that hatred and lusting and lying and stealing were right, but always that hatred and lusting and lying and stealing were wrong.'

The colonel tried to find a flaw in Reverend Mother Auxilia's argument, but even if he had found one, he wouldn't have told Reverend Mother Auxilia, because he was too fond of her. People began to come into the church and to kneel in the pews in front of them, and grave little girls in coloured frocks walked slowly down the aisle with their hands folded.

'And men have always been mocking at priests more because they have dared to preach Christ's message than because they have been afraid to preach it,' Reverend Mother Auxilia went on. 'They have mocked at priests because they themselves did not want to listen to Christ's message, but to disobey it, because life was more comfortable that way. The treason of the laity has been greater than the treason of the clerks, Herr Oberst. But now that the consequences of disobeying God's will are so evident and because their major disobediences of God's will are appearing as though they were going to put an end to their minor disobediences of God's will, men are becoming frightened and asking why the priests have not preached truth more clearly. If they were really Christian they would not be frightened of the end of the world, because if they had led good lives they would know that they were about to see God face to face; no, they are frightened of the sight of the end of the world because they want to go on buying and selling in the market-places.'

'I don't want to go on buying and selling in the market-place, and yet I am frightened of the thought of the end of the world,' Colonel Nicobar said.

'When I was in Rome the Holy Father was saying

three things to me,' Reverend Mother Auxilia said. 'First, he was saying that our Lord had already preached the gospel and that he himself had three hundred thousand priests under his orders trying to make men obey it; secondly, he was saying that we must never forget that our Lord Himself had said that many were called but few were chosen; thirdly, he was saying that our Lord had never promised happiness in this life even to those who obeyed His commands, but only happiness in the next world. Please for us both to be thinking about these three things, Herr Oberst, and then perhaps we shall be humble and content with trying to be good ourselves and to be making others good by our own example.'

Colonel Nicobar still felt that there was a catch in it somewhere and he wanted to ask Reverend Mother Auxilia what the answer was about those who honestly could not accept the divinity of Christ or the truth of the Christian revelation; but a change in Reverend Mother Auxilia's demeanour prevented him. The priest who had been kneeling at the sanctuary rails came out of the sacristy in a clumsy cheap white chasuble and with his unbrushed red hair falling in a lick over his forehead began to say Mass.

When the mystery was over, Reverend Mother Auxilia accompanied the colonel to his car which was waiting outside the church.

'Good-bye, Herr Oberst, and please not to be sad,' she said.

'I don't think I'm sad often really,' the colonel said.

'I am knowing that you are sad, Herr Oberst,' Reverend Mother Auxilia said. 'I am knowing that you are sad because when you are gay it is not you who are gay and I am knowing that Twingo is gay because when he is sad it is not he who is sad.'

'And what's going to be the answer to it all, Reverend Mother?' Colonel Nicobar asked.

'I'm afraid I haven't a sausage,' Reverend Mother Auxilia said.

XXVII

Is my dress all right at the back, dear?' Mrs. Omicron, who had arrived from England that afternoon, asked her husband as she prepared to mount the long staircase at the Kinsky Palace, which wasn't quite as gay as it used to be, even if Operation Henpeck was now known as the Married Families' Scheme.

'A 1 at Lloyd's,' Colonel Omicron said unenthusiastically.

'Now, Humphrey, are you sure you're really looking properly?' Mrs. Omicron asked, shaking out a bunch of black silk. 'Sometimes, dear, I think you don't pay much attention to what I'm saying. I mean your eyes wander, and I've told you time and time again that I like people to listen to me with their eyes as well as with their ears.'

'How in the name of Heaven, Constance, do you expect me to listen to you with my eyes from behind?' Colonel Omicron asked.

'I can *feel* when you're listening with your eyes and when you aren't,' Mrs. Omicron said. 'You seem to forget that woman in Bournemouth told me I was psychic.'

272

'Ha, ha, your aura, what?' Colonel Omicron said.

'There's no need to be rude, Humphrey,' Mrs. Omicron said. 'I was under the impression we had come here to enjoy ourselves, but there you go again, spoiling things as usual.'

'Now look here, Constance, if you're going to start getting unpleasant,' Colonel Omicron said.

'I'm not getting unpleasant, Humphrey; it's you who are *being* unpleasant,' Mrs. Omicron said. 'I'm almost beginning to think that you're sorry I came out to Vienna.'

This was a dangerous topic which Colonel Omicron avoided by not answering his wife's accusation. Instead he manoeuvred her into the bar and steered her skilfully past Audrey, who was standing knocking back pink gins with the Rumanian general, who was now looking for only *sixty* loyal Rumanians. A double sherry seemed to do the trick: Mrs. Omicron stuck her big beak into it with relish.

'This'd cost you a fortune in England,' she said.

'It's not really *given* away over here,' Colonel Omicron said.

'There you go again: being mean, grudging me my enjoyment,' Mrs. Omicron said.

'I'm not grudging you your enjoyment,' Colonel Omicron said. 'Look here, Constance, why will you always persist in misinterpreting my most innocent remarks?'

'They're not innocent remarks; they're insulting

remarks,' Mrs. Omicron said. 'All I can say is, Humphrey, that I hope you haven't been carrying on like those men at the bar with these young girls there. If you ask me my opinion, I think it's positively degrading.'

'Nobody's asking you your opinion, Constance,' Colonel Omicron said.

'Oh, yes, they are, Humphrey: I'm asking myself my opinion,' Mrs. Omicron said. 'Humphrey, I want you to answer me a question: Have you or have you not been demeaning yourself with these fast women?'

'Damn it all, Constance, they're *not* fast women,' Colonel Omicron said.

'Humphrey, have you or have you not been demeaning yourself?' Mrs. Omicron asked.

'Not,' Colonel Omicron said.

'Swear?' Mrs. Omicron said.

'Swear,' Colonel Omicron said.

It was then that Audrey came up to them, swinging her hips and looking luscious.

'At it again, sweetie pie?' she said.

XXVIII

Every day for three weeks Colonel Nicobar had reported to the War Office, but always the reply had been that the general was in Japan and would see him when he returned. With strikes and queues London didn't seem to be what it used to be, and, alone in the crowded empty Christless world of pedigree and chemists' shops, the colonel had more than once almost lost hope. His wife and daughters were in Devon and in the hotel the waitresses were impertinent and the other guests were shockers to look at. This morning, however, when he came down to breakfast he was cheered by the sight of two letters from Vienna: one was from Schwester Kasimira and the other from Sergeant Moonlight; he opened Schwester Kasimira's first. The nun had written in French:

Mon cher colonel,
   Je vous envoie ces quelques mots pour vous dire combien notre communauté regrette votre départ de Vienne. Chaque jour nous prions dans la chapelle, pour que le Bon Dieu vous envoie la lumière. Nous pensons bientôt commencer une neuvaine à cette intention.

Le commandant McPhimister paraît toujours beaucoup souffrir de la cruelle perte qu'il vient de subir en la personne de Maria. Nous prions beaucoup pour lui ainsi que pour elle.

Nous espérons toutes que vous êtes en bonne santé; soignez bien ce précieux don de Dieu.

La Révérende Mère Auxilia me prie de vous saluer bien amic alement de sa part, car elle garde un très bon souvenir de vous.

Veuillez agréer, monsieur le colonel, l'expression de mes meilleurs sentiments en notre Seigneur.

KASIMIRA
Tochter des Heiligen Geistes

At first the colonel was disappointed by the conventional phraseology of the letter, which scarcely seemed to mirror the enchantment of their friendship in Vienna. Were these sterile phrases all that remained of their high convictions and of the Reverend Mother Auxilia's attempt to convert the world? Then he realized that Schwester Kasimira was too simple and holy to have been able to write otherwise, because those who were good at obeying God were not good at talking about it.

Sergeant Moonlight's letter was not quite so spiritual:

Dear Sir,

I am writing this to tell you that I am missing you, sir. Things are not the same since you've gone with Colonel Omicron stamping round the office like a big cheese and never saying good morning or anything. This is not intended to be mutinous, sir, but sometimes I think he's a little too aloft, sir.

I have always admired you, sir, because you are a good soldier. Also because my father looked just like you, sir. My father was a big man and sometimes his language wasn't very idealistic. I don't know what gases there were in him when he died, but he swelled up like a balloon. Fate, ain't it, sir. All the very best wishes, sir.

With kind regards, sir
Yours sincerely
JAMES MOONLIGHT

The colonel folded both letters and put them away in his pocket. At the next table two middle-aged women were talking animatedly about clothing coupons. Three tables further away, a man with grey hair was telling another man with a polished bald head that these ex-officer fellows would have to roll up their sleeves and get down to a hard job of work again if they wanted to earn their living in industry. At another table a willowy young man with wavy hair had interrupted his reading of Immanuel Kant to tell a waitress that he wouldn't have voted Labour if he had known that the new Government wasn't going to increase the marmalade ration. Was this for what Schwester Kasimira had prayed and Sergeant Moonlight risked his life? Perhaps the Pope was right, after all. However hard His Holiness howled, he wouldn't do any good.

277

The human race was hopeless. The only answer seemed to be bigger and better atom bombs.

Outside, it was pouring, great stabs of rain, like knitting needles. The colonel took a taxi to the War Office, chiefly because of the rain.

To his surprise they told him that the general had returned from Japan the previous evening and would see him that morning, so the colonel sat down to wait and to wonder what was going to happen to him. A severe reprimand probably, loss of a pip and a tour of duty in Burma or Scottish Command. A major-general was also waiting to see the general, but he didn't talk to the colonel and sat with a stony unseeing stare, sticking out his lower lip and looking like a baboon. The colonel thought for a little about what he would say to the major-general if he himself were a lieutenant-general. Then the major-general went in to see the general and the colonel began to wonder again about what was going to happen to him.

The major-general was out again almost immediately and walked down the corridor with an important look on his face. Breathing a silent prayer to Schwester Kasimira to pray for him, Colonel Nicobar went in to see the general. The general was chewing his handkerchief, a great big red one with yellow spots.

'Ah, Nicobar,' the general greeted and did not seem too angry. 'Of course, I remember. Cousin

278

of that chap in the Sixtieth who stole that Spalding Midget from me in 1912. Yes, yes, I'm still chewing handkerchiefs, but it's quilts my wife gets waxy about. Says they're irreplaceable. We're living in the country now, you know. Of course, I haven't been there since I got back, but I hope to get down for week-ends. Quite a decent little estate with a small pond too. My wife says I ought to drain the pond because it always keeps overflowing and messing up the garden, but I say where on earth would I put all my old razor blades?' His tone suddenly became official: 'The subject, Nicobar, is conversive activities.'

'*Sub*versive activities, you mean, don't you, sir?' Colonel Nicobar said.

'No, I don't Nicobar,' the general said. 'I mean *con*versive activities. You see, Nicobar, we're reforming the army, getting rid of old shibboleths and outworn customs, letting chaps read in bed and not go to church, in short, making the army the opposite of what it used to be. And I've decided to put you in charge of the operation.'

'Thank you, sir, but . . .' the colonel said.

'Please do not interrupt me, Nicobar, until I've finished speaking,' the general said. 'I can't tell you how much I admired that stunt of yours pinching my topcoat in Vienna. Showed an originality of thought and a preference for unorthodox methods which is entirely commendable. And all to get a nun to Rome so that she could have a chin-wag with the Pope. A little bit against modern thought, perhaps, you know, spirit of the times, and all that, but the method was admirable. And in modern warfare, it's method that counts, initiative, tenacity of purpose. Well, you're going to get your reward. I'm going to send you on a world tour and you'll start off as a brigadier.'

'But, sir . . .' Colonel Nicobar said.

'Look here, Nicobar, it's no use your telling me that you didn't take that topcoat on purpose,' the general said testily. 'I know that's the tale you told that dim bulb Catlock, but it won't wash with me. And in any case I've made up my mind that you're the man for the job. And once I've made up my mind about anything, nothing can alter my decision. Look here, Nicobar. Don't you understand? I'm *wanting* you to have taken that topcoat on purpose. Come, come, you did take it on purpose, didn't you?'

Trying not to think of Schwester Kasimira, Colonel Nicobar remembered what Reverend Mother Auxilia had said in the aeroplane about her Holy Founder, Saint Walburga of Graz, not letting him down. There might be more in all this than met the eye. He grinned slowly at the general. After all, he might as well be promoted for a sheep as for a lamb.

THE END